AUSTEN, PARTY OF TWO

A PRIDE & PREJUDICE RETELLING

BRITNEY M. MILLS

CRYSTAL CANYON PUBLISHING

CHAPTER 1

If Lexi Sarmiento had more than a few muffins and pastries left over, she'd probably keep her food truck open longer, but then she would never hear the end of it. Family parties were non-negotiable for her mom and she was already late as it was.

It took a few scrubs, but she finally got the syrup off the counter. She pulled the sliding window down, ending business for the day. The sun had nearly set, signaling how late she was without looking at her phone. She picked up her pace, placing the caramel and chocolate sauce bottles back by the powdered sugar shaker in the see-through plastic box on the counter.

It was unlike her to be late for even a dental appointment, but business for her food truck hadn't slowed down for most of the day.

She placed the unsold pastries in a large pink box, locked up the truck, and headed down the road toward her apartment. The box was awkward for the several blocks distance, and she had to adjust it several times, holding it against her hip or on her shoulder. At one point, she wondered why she even bothered to bring it at all.

The sidewalks were busy for eight o'clock on a weeknight, and no matter how fast she tried to walk, she always got stuck behind the slowest person. She wished she could snap her fingers and be there already. As exciting as it was to have a killer sale day, she'd dealt with enough people over the past twelve hours, and all she wanted was a tub and a week of sleep.

The bell on the door rang as she walked into her parents' Italian-Peruvian restaurant in the North End. The front was empty, but she heard voices coming from the event room in the back. She hoisted the box on her shoulder and moved in that direction, finding the room lit up, bright-colored paper and decorations hung all over the walls in celebration. There were two paper banners, one reading Happy Birthday and the other Feliz Cumpleaños, all set up for her older sister's birthday.

Lexi grinned, thinking of the time when she was around thirteen and had asked why they had to have both banners. She'd gotten a prompt tap on the head with a spoon and the lecture to never forget her heritage.

The room was full of people, most of whom were related to the Sarmiento family. Comparing, eating food, talking loudly. It wouldn't be a normal family get-together if those three things didn't take place.

"Happy Birthday, Ceila!" she called, seeing her sister walking in her direction. She set the box down on the table overflowing with food and wrapped her sister in a hug. "I hope it's been a great day for you."

Ceila turned to the table, adding several small scoops of food from the numerous options. When she saw Lexi just standing there, she pointed to the stack of plates for Lexi to do the same.

"I've had a really good day. I got a pedicure, read part of a new book Mami and Papi gave me." She stood back from the table, stabbing a piece of shrimp and placing it into her mouth. With a plate full of her favorites, Lexi waited for her sister to finish.

"It's about time you showed up. You look exhausted. Long day?" Ceila's eyes danced around, inspecting every part of her. As much as it irritated Lexi, her sister's intuitiveness kept her sane, always knowing what to ask and how to take care of those around her.

"Long but good. I didn't have time to calculate the numbers, but I think I broke my record."

Ceila smiled. "Didn't you just do that a couple of months ago?"

Lexi set her face in a pout. "Yes, but it's always nice to make progress, don't you think? How are things with you?"

Her sister shrugged. "Same old thing, I guess. Richard is late too. He's been so off lately, like distant. Do I break up with him?"

"Do you love him?" Lexi knew how much her sister loved her boyfriend, but the pain of rejection was ever present. Dating hadn't gone well in the past few years for the two oldest of the five Sarmiento sisters. Doubts plagued them when the smallest things were off in their relationships.

She closed her eyes, and leaning her head on Lexi's shoulder, Ceila sighed. "You know I do. Maybe I'm just overreacting. It's hard not to when Mami is always talking about why you and I aren't married yet."

"Your track record is already better than mine. Richard's a good guy too, the best guy you've dated so far. Maybe he's planning something exciting."

"I hope so."

Lexi turned to the food table and waved her hand over it. "There's so much food here, it looks like we haven't even made a dent." She smiled, motioning to the box of pastries. "I saved you a cronut."

"You love me," Ceila said, her eyes wide as she wrapped Lexi in another hug. "You better finish your food. I'm sure Mami will have us eating the cake soon."

Lexi raised her eyebrow, searching the table for the cake. "Cake? I thought you didn't want one this year. No one even asked me to make it. Where did they get it?"

Ceila grimaced, as if wishing she could take back the words. "Mike's down the street. Mami thought you'd be too busy with everything going on at the food truck."

Irritation bubbled in Lexi's stomach, causing her to grit her teeth. "Just because they didn't want me to buy the truck, doesn't mean I'm too busy to make my own sister's birthday cake. I've been doing it for the last few years."

Their mother's voice echoed through the crowd of people, and Ceila straightened.

"I guess I better mingle, since I am the birthday girl. Mami will go crazy if I haven't had a thirty-minute discussion with each guest." She took a bite of the cronut and sighed, closing her eyes and smiling wide. Spots of the pink frosting stuck around the corners of her mouth. "You're the best. Ever." She gave Lexi a quick hug and moved away.

Lexi was tempted to turn around and walk back out, the betrayal slicing through her chest. Sure, things had been a little crazy the past several months as she'd spent most of her time trying to get the truck to turn a profit, but she still cared deeply about her family. Why her mother hadn't wanted her to make the cake irritated her more than she cared to admit.

Her stomach grumbled, reminding her she hadn't eaten since the dry toast she'd snagged on her way out the door that morning.

Holding her plate with both hands so it wouldn't collapse under the mountain of food, her eyes darted around, looking for a seat and keeping an eye out for her mother. All the usual family members were there, and she didn't feel like talking to anyone yet. They'd inevitably ask about her lack of boyfriend and what she was doing to remedy the situation. With her parents, the argument usually formed around their dislike of her food truck, and the best way to keep the peace was to avoid having to talk about it.

When she found a seat at the end of a table, she sat and dug in. It was times like these when she was grateful for her parents' cooking. The combination of pasta and seasoned meats hit the spot, especially after a double shift when her sole employee Sarai, had called in sick today. Sitting felt like a day at the spa for her aching feet and lower back, but that meant another successful day. She couldn't complain about that.

"Can I sit by you, Lexi?" a small voice asked next to her. Lexi turned to see one of her younger cousins Marisol, smiling at her.

"Of course, Mari. How are things in the second grade?"

Marisol grinned and shook her head. "I only have two more weeks, and I'll be in third grade. Well, after the summer anyway."

"I can't believe you're getting so big. You need to tell your mom to bring you to the food truck so I can spoil you with sweets." Lexi giggled when Marisol's eyes went wide, her head bobbing up and down in agreement.

"When you don't have to work, will you come take me to the park again? It's always so much fun when you go." Marisol's words called up a memory for Lexi of the last time they'd gone to the park. It had been a month or two after Garrett had left, and she'd needed a distraction. Armed with a bag of sand toys, they'd spent a few hours creating a large castle and almost a complete village before one of the boys had stomped through it.

Lexi tapped her nose. "I would love to. I'll let your mom know when that is."

Tia Angela called for Marisol to go find her younger sister, leaving Lexi alone for a few seconds.

Someone slid a plate down on the table across from her, and Lexi glanced up to register who it was before concentrating on her food again.

"What do you want, Sophie?" She heard the annoyance in her voice and stuffed a bite into her mouth before she said more.

Only two years younger than Lexi, she seemed older with her more refined personality and manners. Where Lexi barely hit over five feet, her sister was at least six inches taller. Sophie's hair was a dark brown, where Lexi's was a natural shade of jet black. She often held tightly to the opinions of their mother, meaning her presence at the table threw off the happiness she'd had with Marisol.

Sophie's clasped hands tipped Lexi off that something was going on. She'd wring them so tight when she was nervous, or even excited, that her knuckles turned white, something she'd done as long as Lexi could remember.

When she didn't say anything, her expression confirmed Lexi's gut feeling that something was about to happen, but she wouldn't like it. Would it be something about the food truck or that their mother had invited a "special guest" over for Lexi to meet?

Sophie gave her a slight smile and said, "Well, um, I wanted to wish you luck on your—"

"Alexis, when did you get here?" Their mother's voice floated over to them, its sickly sweet tone alerting her to some scheme.

Lexi took a bite of the fries from the lomo saltado and said, "Just now, Mami."

"Oh, Alexis. Don't speak with your mouth full. No wonder you don't have a boyfriend."

Ouch. Her life summed up in a single sentence in her mother's eyes. She was getting used to her mother's insults about relationships but every once in a while, the jabs sank deeper. But she'd never tell her mother that.

A young man moved behind Angelica Sarmiento, his bright blond hair and light complexion standing out in the room full of dark hair and dark eyes. His smile was forced, liked he'd been brought here against his will.

"Who's this?" Lexi asked.

Her mother turned and put her hand on the guy's arm, smiling wider than Lexi had seen in some time. It was the "Be nice" kind of smile that threatened to take all the fun out of life if she didn't obey. Lexi smiled as she remembered the day she turned sixteen. She was by no means a rebel, but that smile no longer held sway.

"This is Aaron Shaw. He's the son of the restaurant owners down the street. He's just home for summer break, and we got to talking down at the market earlier today. With you being single and him not dating anyone, I wanted you two to meet."

Because that's logical. He's single, I'm single. A match made in heaven. Not. There was no way this guy was even close to her type, and his baby face made him look like he should still be in high school.

Lexi nodded, working to keep her eyes from rolling. "It's nice to meet you." She looked back at her food and took another bite, savoring the tenderness of the meat while calming her annoyance.

"Alexis, that's not how we treat our guests," her mother said through clenched teeth, her eyes flashing. Lexi returned it with a challenging glare. In a quick movement, her mother pulled her up from her seat, dragging her out of the room.

She stopped in the hall that led to the kitchen of their restaurant, letting go of Lexi's arm.

"What is wrong with you?" Her mother's face flushed, her eyes wild.

"Are you really asking me that right now? First, you didn't ask me to make the cake. And second—"

Her mother threw her hands up in the air. "We've hardly seen you, hija. We just figured you'd be too busy to make it."

She wanted to react, to step inches away from her mother and yell in her face. But she hadn't been brought up to disrespect her parents, and with a crowd in the next room, she had to try a different approach.

"That's what a phone is for, Mami. I would have made time to make it. Just because you didn't want me to bake and cook—"

Her mother's face turned hard. "Don't go putting this all on us. You know what it's like growing up in a restaurant. We've never traveled anywhere, and we hardly get time with all the family together without work getting in the way. I wanted to spare you from it, but you're as stubborn as your father."

"Well, in the future, please ask me first. My family is my biggest priority." Lexi's hands had emphasized every word, never breaking her gaze from her mother's face.

"Why can't your future family be at the top of your list?" Her mother's arms were folded across her chest, her head cocked to one side, staring at Lexi with an 'I-know-what's-best' look.

A growl surged in her throat, and Lexi turned away from her mother, wishing she could just march right back out of the building. "If you weren't trying to set me up with the high school student down the road, maybe I could focus energy on dating. Mami, I can find a guy on my own." She hated how much her voice sounded like she was pleading.

With hands on hips, her mother narrowed her eyes. "All you do is work at that truck. You never go out. You only have that one baking friend Charlotte. I wish you'd go do something with your life."

"I am, Ma. I'm running my own business, just like you and Papi."

"But you could have been a lawyer or something better than *just* a baker." Her mother's face puckered, like she tasted something sour.

Shaking her head, Lexi wanted to yell. Instead, she dropped her voice to just above a whisper. "I tried that, Mami. Baking is my passion. The truck is doing well, and I love it. I wish you'd come see it instead of judge me from five streets away."

Why do I even try to talk to them about this? It was the same argument every few weeks, one she might never win.

"Just be nice to Aaron. Go on a date. If it doesn't work out, well, I'm not sure what to do with you." Tears formed in her mother's eyes. "I just want grandkids before I die, hija."

Lexi wasn't fooled by the act. "Why can't you pester Kathy and Jacqueline about their life choices a little more too? They run around like they own the world, and we all have to suffer the consequences."

The room behind them went quiet, and Lexi took two steps toward the door to see what was going on. Lexi saw Ceila's boyfriend Richard, down on one knee. That answered the question of why he'd been distant. Lexi moved forward, her heart pounding and her lungs squeezed, hoping her sister was getting engaged.

She'd missed the first part of the speech but heard the most important line. "I love you, Ceila. Will you marry me?" Lexi glanced to Ceila, her sister's hands covering her face as her eyes welled up with tears. She only nodded, pulling him up to kiss him long on the lips.

"I didn't expect that." Surprised by the nearness of the voice, Lexi turned to see Aaron standing next to her, his arms crossed over his body.

"You and me both." She bit her lip. "How old are you, Aaron?"

"Twenty-two."

Awesome. Only a six-year gap. Thank you, Ma.

"Did my mother pay you or something to go on a date with me?" Lexi cocked her head, studying his reaction.

"No, well, not in that way. I mean, she did give me a little money to use on a date. But I—"

Lexi raised a hand to stop him, shaking her head. "You're good. I'm used to it by now." She walked over to her purse and pulled out her wallet. "Here is forty dollars. Go do something fun with it, no strings attached."

Aaron's eyes brightened, and he grabbed the cash from her. "You'll be okay then?"

"Yeah, I think I'll be all right. Go find some girl your own age." Lexi chuckled. "And if my mom tries to set you up with any of my other sisters, just run. Better yet, if you see her coming in your direction, just hide." The expression on Aaron's face was a mixture of fear and confusion.

"Uh, thank you. This has got to be the weirdest thing that's ever happened to me."

Lexi patted his shoulder and walked a few steps with him toward the door. "I promise, not every family is like mine. Good luck, Aaron." He dodged out the door like the building was suddenly on fire.

Laughing, Lexi made her way back to her plate of food. She glanced at Ceila but couldn't find her in the swarm of people congratulating her. What she did was start the downward tumble of her ego as she connected eyes with her Aunt Sylvia. The woman was as irritating as Lexi's mom. She'd have to squeal with her sister later.

A text came through as she picked up her fork and plate, ducking out of the room and into the kitchen. Her best friend Charlotte. Swiping to see the full message, she was ready to throw her phone.

Will you come to a speed dating event with me tomorrow?

No. Lexi tapped send and took another bite of chicken. Did no one else think of anything but relationships?

Her ringtone sounded. For a second, she thought about sending her friend straight to voicemail. Knowing Charlotte wouldn't give up, she answered.

"What?"

"Wow. You're in a great mood tonight. Someone break your favorite rolling pin?"

Lexi burst out laughing. "How long have you been waiting to use that one, Char?"

"Not long. It just came to me. Anywho, how strongly are you willing to keep your best friend duties?"

"If you say going speed dating is one of those duties, I might have to find another best friend." Leaning her arm on the table, Lexi closed her eyes, waiting for Charlotte's convincing, more like guilt-ridden, speech.

"You can do me a huge favor, and I know it would make you feel better." Charlotte paused, probably trying to see how Lexi would react.

Sitting in front of fifteen strangers while saying the same information over and over wasn't something that would make her feel better.

"My mom just tried to set me up with a twenty-two-year-old, so if this speed dating event allows eighteen-year-olds and up, I'm out. I don't need to waste my time on someone who doesn't remember the singers of this century, let alone the classics." She breathed in deeply and let the air go a little at a time, taking some of the stress with it. "I'm sorry. It's been a day, and my emotions have been all over the place."

Charlotte sighed. "I'm sorry, girl. But that's a good reason to go with me. You can tell your mom you're trying, and maybe she'll back off." She and Lexi laughed at the same time, knowing that wouldn't appease Angelica in the slightest. Not until there was a ring on Lexi's finger. "It's put on by that matchmaking company downtown, Love, Austen, so I doubt you'll have to worry about eighteen-year-olds. It will be so much better if I'm there with you. Please? Please? If I were at your house, I'd be down on a knee begging."

"I've already seen that today."

"Huh?"

"Richard proposed to Ceila." She scraped at her plate and stood to throw it into the garbage can, waiting for Charlotte's cheer to die down.

"That's so exciting. Ceila deserves to be happy after some of the losers she's put up with," Charlotte said.

Lexi nodded. That was an understatement. Ceila had dated a man the year before who'd taken just about all of Ceila's life savings and disappeared to some tropical island. The last they'd heard from the police was that he'd been conning people all around Boston before disappearing.

"Do you have everything settled for the bake-off?" It was the perfect change of subject.

"Yes." Charlotte's curt tone mirrored a teenager going out for the night.

"Okay, well, I just thought I'd offer to help. Being one of the advice givers doesn't seem like that much work." Charlotte's family owned a large facility that was essentially a cooking school. The month before, Charlotte had asked for Lexi to be one of the judges/coaches for an upcoming competition they were holding at the school. Lexi had watched her fair share of reality shows and was excited to help.

"Just wait until you see the students. It won't be easy, that's for sure."

"Eh, piece of cake." The baking joke caused them both to laugh aloud, and Lexi saw her mother pop her head around the doorway, frowning. Lexi ducked down, walking deeper into the kitchen.

"So, will you come?"

Remembering the big order she had to have for tomorrow, Lexi groaned. When Meg, the owner for Love, Austen, had called to ask for an assortment of pastries for an event she had planned, Lexi was just grateful it wasn't another huge dinner, like the gala she'd catered two weeks before. She'd need more time before she did that again.

Lexi sighed. "I have to bring the refreshments for it, so I'll stick around for a bit longer. But if things get weird, I'm out." Throwing her plate in the garbage, she said, "I'll just meet you there." Maybe she'd make an appearance and then leave before the activity began. There was no way she'd find someone real at a speed dating event.

CHAPTER 2

I've got the perfect person to line you up with

Brennen Peters shook his head and set the phone back on his dresser. His sister Clara, was always trying to set him up with someone.

Not going to happen.

He thought about the last blind date his sister had "accidentally" invited him to and then conveniently left, leaving him alone and unprepared for a date. With a quick rub to his wet hair with a towel, the soreness was already tightening his shoulders.

He'd pushed himself harder in his workout today than he had in a few weeks, and sore muscles were already taking over his body. It had been at least a month since he'd uploaded a new workout to his app, Fitness Overhaul, and he was glad he had something new to share with his followers.

She's amazing. At least give her a chance.

He thought about sending a response, but knowing his sister, she wouldn't give up. Best to give her space and get to work.

Sitting at his desk, he flipped through the notes section

on his phone where he kept track of the restaurants he'd been to and ones he still needed to try. His side job was critiquing restaurants for the local newspaper, which seemed like a contradiction since he'd made most of his money helping people slim down with workouts that mixed lifting, cardio, and stretching.

There were times he wished he'd learned how to cook, but he'd survived at least nine years without home-cooked food. The app and the constant need to think of new workouts helped him stay in shape, or he'd probably have a gut already. Cheat meals at some of Boston's best restaurants made it worth all the sacrifices of sleep.

His phone rang. Scott Goff, his editor at the Boston World.

"Hey, Scott. How are you?" He leaned back, lifting his legs up to rest on the desk.

"Your latest article has lost your edge." The curt response stabbed at Brennen's ego, and he took a breath, knowing the man was usually right about things like this.

I'm doing well, thanks.

Brennen rubbed his forehead, hoping to stave off any headaches before noon on a Friday. "What do you mean by that, sir?" He'd learned at the beginning of his time as a writer for the newspaper that it was better to respect the editor's age. His mother would've been happy about that.

"It doesn't have that grit your reviews usually do. I need it to tell a story, and this one doesn't."

"Look, Scott. I know you wanted me to cover some food trucks that are popping up around town, but there isn't much to write about." Brennen scrunched his nose at the idea. He'd always been one for a sit-down restaurant, a place where he could leave his worries about life at the door and enjoy a good meal. Food trucks only added to the stress of life, making it difficult to eat since there were no real tables.

They perpetuated busy, making it convenient for businessmen and women to grab something while they hurried off to their next appointment.

Scott cleared his throat, the sound echoing through the line. "There's always something to write about. You'll need to think outside the box. I wouldn't mind if you said you hated them. Just give the piece some substance."

"When I do my usual reviews, I'm inside. The ambience of the restaurant helps formulate part of the review. I can comment on the waiter's attentiveness, on the cleanliness of the room, speed of service."

"Focus on the truck and the food. So, you don't have all that fluff to work with. Your last ten reviews have all been positive. People are getting bored, Brennen. If you didn't like the place, say so."

"Food trucks aren't restaurants."

A deep chuckle came through the line, and Brennen smiled. At least he'd gotten the older man to laugh. "Write about it. You're going to get flak from that point of view but run with it. I expect the rewrite by end of day today."

The line went dead, and Brennen pulled the phone back, staring at the floor-to-ceiling bookshelves on the wall opposite him. So many books he'd collected, but he'd only made it through a handful of them. Who knew writing would make it difficult to find time for reading?

He rarely had a hard time reviewing restaurants. As he thought more about it, the last few reviews had felt the same. But there were so many moving parts at a restaurant. At a food truck, he felt like he was attacking the owner because they didn't have many employees.

Pulling up the document of the draft he'd sent to Scott, Brennen read over it again, understanding what his editor had meant about the difference in tone. Highlighting everything, he pushed delete.

The black cursor on the blank screen seemed to taunt him and he switched over to his inbox, hoping to get inspiration by taking his mind off it.

* * *

TWO HOURS LATER, the bell from the front door rang, causing Brennen to jump. The house had been so silent that he'd been too engrossed in his work. Who would come over this early in the day?

He hesitated and stood, moving through his office to the door. Peeking through the window at the side of the door, he saw Parker, one of his best friends.

What is he doing here? Parker never came to his house. This early in the morning, he was usually at his law firm, prepping for his next big case. With his caseload and desire to make partner, they hadn't seen each other outside their Saturday morning rows on the Charles River.

"Hey, man. What are you doing here at noon? Don't you have some marital fight to referee?"

Parker's laugh caused Brennen to echo it. "I have a client meeting in this neighborhood and wanted to make sure you were still alive."

"What do you mean 'still alive?' I work from home. It's the best job a guy could ask for." Brennen waved him in, walking toward the kitchen. "Can I get you a drink or anything?"

He opened the refrigerator and saw a couple of cans of soda, his one indulgence every so often, some lettuce, and cheese. Making a mental note, he'd have to go to the store to get more fruits and veggies.

Parker waved it off. "I can't stay long. The real reason I'm here is I wanted to see if you can be my wingman tonight." He gave Brennen a lopsided grin.

"Since when do you need a wingman?" Brennen took a

glass from one of his cupboards, holding it up to the water dispenser on the door of his fridge.

"Since two minutes ago. I could use a bottled water. Do you have one in here?" Parker opened the fridge. His mouth dropped open, and he turned to Brennen, motioning to the fridge. "Really? All you have is lettuce and cheese in here. How do you eat?"

Brennen opened a different cupboard, exposing two large tubs of protein powder. "I don't cook, so I eat out. It was just easier since..." he trailed off, not wanting to finish the sentence. It hurt too much.

"Yeah, I know. But a few more groceries go a long way." Parker shut the fridge and leaned over the large island. "So, are you free tonight?"

Tonight. Takeout. Sox game.

"Define free." Brennen smirked as he took a sip of the cool water.

Parker walked toward the door. "I'll text you the address. Be there just before seven."

"I haven't said yes. I don't even know what it is."

"You can miss one Sox game. It won't kill you."

As the information processed through Brennen's brain, he remembered something from a recent conversation with Parker. "Wait, whatever happened to matchmaker girl? I thought you were into her."

Parker hesitated and smiled. "I'm late for this meeting, so I'll tell you about it tonight. Just come and help me out."

"Fine." He could have said no, could have come up with a bunch of other excuses. But he was curious, and a night out would be good for him.

Brennen walked to the door, and Parker left, the silence settling on the house like an old blanket. As Brennen thought what he'd just agreed to, anxiety took over. But if Parker were the one the girls would focus on tonight, he might survive it. He just hoped it wasn't another lame bar.

Bringing the glass of water with him, he sat behind his desk once again. The cursor blinked a couple more times before he swiped his hand across the keyboard. The result was a mess of letters and symbols, but it did the trick to rid him of the blank page. He sat forward, the words pouring out with ease now.

He'd have to remember that for the next time writer's block hit. If only it were that easy to start a relationship.

CHAPTER 3

The clock on the dashboard said five after seven as Lexi maneuvered her parents' van through the crowded streets. Charlotte wouldn't be happy about her being late but at least she'd shown up, right?

This was the second time in two days she hadn't arrived early to events. Her punctuality was suffering, and she needed to fix it, or she'd have permanent knots in her stomach.

As she pulled up to the address, she realized it was for the restaurant she used to work in, La Crème. Although she'd left on good terms six months ago, but there were still several of her co-workers who thought she was crazy for giving up working at one of the city's top restaurants to own a food truck. It seemed to be a popular sentiment these days as her mind called up an image of her mother.

She carried a large tray of mini desserts, shifting the weight of it to open the door. The same familiar smell and bustling rushed back to her, calling up memories as she'd worked her way up to sous chef. Setting the tray down on the large prep island, she turned to head back out for the next one when a familiar voice echoed through the room.

"I never thought I'd see you back here!" Lexi turned to face Tonya, forcing a smile.

"Hello, Tonya." They'd begun in the same cooking school and had competed up until Lexi had quit, allowing Tonya to take her spot in the kitchen. Lexi continued back to the doors, waving for a few other employees to follow her.

"How's the food truck business? Taking on other jobs to help you get by?" Her snide tone was the last thing Lexi needed to worry about tonight.

She pulled the tray from the van and handed it to one of the workers, repeating the action until she was the last one left to take anything. There was no way she would chance Tonya holding fifty desserts that she'd spent hours making.

"The food truck is going really well actually," she said, keeping her tone even. "I just accepted a catering job for a friend. How's life at La Crème? Do you miss me?"

Tonya's mouth parted slightly, irritation written on her face.

Lexi placed her tray on the island and turned to see John, the prepper, nod his head vigorously behind her back. That was answer enough.

"It's good to see you all. I'd love to stay and chat, but I'm already late. The place looks great, as always." Why Meg hadn't just ordered from the restaurant itself, Lexi didn't know. They had some of the best desserts in the city, but a surge of pride rose that Meg believed in her. At least someone did.

As she moved to the doors between the kitchen and the restaurant, butterflies invaded her stomach. She stood behind the swinging door, moving once a waiter came through with a tray.

Will I survive tonight?

Maybe she could find someone who'd be up for a fake relationship. That way, her mother and Charlotte would leave her alone. Surely there was someone here desperate enough to agree to that. She'd seen it done in the movies and while she knew the plot to all of them, she figured she wouldn't make the same mistakes.

On second thought, that would be harder than just being single. And she didn't tolerate lying. Period. As scary as parts of life were, she did her best to be honest about it. She never had to watch her back or try to remember what she'd said and to whom.

Opening her large shoulder bag, she pulled out a pair of white heels, switching out her flats. It took a minute for her feet to adjust to the four-inch stilettos her mother insisted she wear. To Angelica Sarmiento, the way to catch a man's eye was through his stomach and by wearing stilts.

After a breath, she walked in and to the left. The server entrance into the large room made it easy for her to slip in unnoticed. The familiar scents of garlic, oregano, parmesan, and baking bread filled her nose. The lights in the restaurant were dim, giving the room a more intimate feel. Several people milled around the bar, probably hoping to make tonight easier if they were joining the speed dating event.

The hostess directed her to the back of the restaurant where she found dozens of small tables, a chair on one side with a booth on the other. The panic surged in her chest, and she breathed in and out slowly, leaning up against a wall. Not only were there so many memories swirling through her, she didn't know if she could take all those rejections at once. As her dating life went now, she'd been on a date maybe once or twice a year, and that was bad enough.

"You made it!" Charlotte said, greeting her from the other side of the room. She'd been talking to a few other girls, each one as dolled up as they could be. Dressed in a powder-blue dress that fell to her knees, Charlotte's soft, blond curls fell over one shoulder in a side ponytail. The amount of makeup on her face was more than Lexi was used to seeing on her.

She must be hoping to find someone tonight. Lexi saw the hope in her eyes and felt bad she hadn't recognized it before. She'd been focused on her business and everything but men. Thinking of Charlotte's life, she probably didn't have many chances to meet a decent guy. She'd taken over the family baking school, and most of the people who came to her classes were women and already married men. Straightening, she could support her friend, even if it were to endure this painful night.

"You look lovely," Lexi said, giving her friend a hug.

"You do too. Definitely sporting the Lexi style." Charlotte grinned at her, and Lexi rolled her eyes. The other girls in the group laughed, and Lexi saw one girl's nose turn up.

"You look like my grandmother in high school. What time period are you supposed to be from? The Regency era?" The girl's high-pitched sneer was nothing Lexi hadn't heard before.

Lexi opened her eyes as wide as possible and cocked her head to the side, ready for the challenge. "The forties, actually. War time, strong women."

The girl pursed her lips and shook her head quickly back and forth, as if that were insult enough.

Please don't let her sit next to me.

Focusing on Charlotte, she asked, "So, what are we supposed to do? The sight of these tables almost made me run from the room." Her chuckle sounded forced to her own ears.

"I'm surprised you missed the registration table. Did you come through that door?"

Lexi turned and saw several women bent over a table

near the door leading to the floor of the restaurant. "Nope. I came through the back way."

"You'll sign up over there, and the guy will give you a name tag and a little packet of coupons for random stuff." Lexi noticed the sticker on Charlotte's dress, her beautiful swirly writing stating her name. "Come find me when you're through the line." Her friend turned back to the small group, and Lexi was glad to go. She'd never been good at girl talk.

She stood behind two women in line at the table, her heart pounding in her ears. Why did the thought of dating scare her so much? Maybe because she was attracted to the losers, the ones with all the charm and none of the work ethic or life goals she had. She didn't need to be belittled by a man for her dreams. Or a woman about her style.

Today was a new day though, right? And Lexi was ultimately here for Charlotte, even though it looked like her best friend wasn't worried about this at all.

She glanced around the room, taking in the familiar muted colors and décor. The one table closest to her still had a large scratch in the wood from some angry customers when Lexi had been working there. She hadn't seen it, but she'd heard about it from all the waiters.

Focusing on the table covered with several regular-sized papers, as well as some colored smaller bits, her mind went back to dating.

How did people make it past the first date? The question had eluded her for far too long. She used to worry about it, back in high school and college. And she thought she'd figured it out with Garrett, but when that didn't work out, her attitude changed. When she bought the food truck, her brain had to think so much on the baking and business end of things. There wasn't even a slice of it open to worry about men.

She stepped up to the table, a dark-haired guy smiled at her. "I didn't think I'd ever see you at an event like this."

Lexi nodded, her lips revealing a tight smile. "Parker. What are you doing here?" A trickle of relief started in her shoulders and worked its way down her back. It was always nice to see someone familiar when she was dreading something.

"I came to help Meg out. Tiffany had to go out of town. I'm excited you're here though. Did you come with a friend?" Parker took his eyes from hers to survey the room, as if he'd know them.

"Yes. Charlotte dragged me along. This isn't my first option of how to spend a Friday night. Looks like it's not yours either." She laughed as she pointed to the ear bud in his ear.

A guilty look crossed his face, and then he smiled. "Red Sox game and time with my girl. Best of both worlds."

"What's the score?" She loved how Boston supported their teams, and she followed along as best she could, given her crazy schedule.

Parker leaned over, looking back and forth like they were part of a conspiracy. "Bottom of the first, still no score."

With a hand on her hip, she smiled at him. "If you see me trying to get your attention, you're to come and inform me of the score and tell me someone is waiting at the front door, got it?"

Throwing his head back, Parker howled. "That's a good one. But if Meg ever found out I did that, I'd be gutted. So as much as I like our friendship," he said, pointing between him and Lexi, "I don't want to be back in the dating pool ever again."

She flashed him a sly smile and said, "Well, then you better start looking at rings."

With a wave of his hand, he frowned. "Now, now, we just

started dating for real. And when we're ready, I've got my grandmother's ring to propose with." His words made Lexi audibly sigh. She loved a good love story, and the fact he would use a family heirloom to propose made it that much better.

"Okay, we've got people coming in. Just fill this out with your information," he said, handing her an information sheet. As she filled it out, he slid over a tag like Charlotte's. "Put your name on this tag and then hang out until we get started." She took a pen and filled out her email when she heard Parker say, "Brennen. I'm glad you made it."

By the time Lexi had finished filling out her address, phone number, and email, she turned, and a guy standing behind her caught her eye.

His chestnut hair was short, the top styled in the latest fashion. He wore a button-up shirt and some dark jeans. Everything about him said he didn't want to be there. But Lexi had to mentally tell herself to turn away. Unlike Aaron, this was the kind of guy who checked all her boxes.

Mentally scolding herself for even thinking that, she finished up the info sheet and took her name sticker with her as she walked back to Charlotte. Ogling a guy at a speed dating event was the wrong way to find guys she didn't need in her life.

*B*rennen paused outside the restaurant. He'd changed his course twice on the way there, almost convincing himself that Parker would understand him staying at home to watch the Red Sox play. But Brennen already owed him for helping with a legal jam for an issue with Fitness Overhaul, and if this would help return the favor, he'd put his head down and hope to make it through the night. At least the focus wouldn't be on him.

At a block away, he recognized the place as La Crème, one of the nicer restaurants downtown. He'd attended the opening the year before but hadn't been back since the wait list was months out. Scott had pulled a few strings to get him in for a review the first time.

How am I supposed to be a wingman here?

A bar or a club was one thing, as they could approach a woman without looking creepy. A restaurant? Most women would be here with someone, meaning chances of a date were slim. A prickle rolled up his spine. Something wasn't right.

He parked in the closest public parking garage and took

his time to walk the two blocks to the restaurant, taking deep breaths as he focused on calm. His mind ran through a few of the typical bits of conversation people usually bring up on first dates, having to prep himself to listen and respond accordingly.

The air was warm, and the sun still shone on that part of the city. He was grateful he hadn't opted to wear a jacket in the warm May night. Stepping up to the main door of La Crème, he opened it, a smell of garlic and basil penetrating his nose. The hostess looked up and smiled.

"Name?"

"Um, it should be under Matthews?"

The girl ran her finger down a tablet in front of her. "Are you here for the speed dating event?"

His stomach dropped as if jumping off a fifteen-story building. He knew she was right, but he wanted her to be wrong. "No. I don't think so. My friend Parker Matthews just said to show up here."

"Oh, he said you'd be coming." The girl flashed him a coy smile and said, "Right this way. You're with the party in the back."

This better not be some setup. I'll kill him.

The girl walked straight toward a room at the back of the restaurant, a sign sitting outside that said, "Love, Austen Speed Dating Event." The 'o' in love was even a daisy. She stopped at the door, pointing to the registration table. He stopped at the entrance. What had he agreed to?

His body tingled with the anger humming inside. Parker knew he wasn't ready for a relationship, might never be ready. Everyone around him said his standards for a girl were too high. But if that kept him from getting hurt, he wouldn't lower them for anyone less.

With a glance to the left, he saw Parker behind a large table, smiling up at a girl in a red polka dot dress. She had to be barely five feet tall subtracting the size of her heels. She looked like she was almost en pointe in ballet slippers, except for the heel on them could probably do some damage if needed. They couldn't be comfortable. Her black hair sat in a high ponytail, and he could see her delicate features from her profile.

"Brennen," Parker said. His voice sounded a little off at first but gained confidence. "I'm glad you could make it. Sign this paper, and I'll get you a name tag."

The woman looked back at him for a moment, her milk chocolate eyes mesmerizing. His gaze broke away and drifted to her red lips, keeping his attention until she turned back to Parker. She handed him the paper and moved away from the table.

Brennen thrust a hand into his pocket, willing himself not to watch her walk away. He didn't need any more reason to stay here and if Parker saw him, he'd try to set things up.

Staring at the top of his friend's head, he waited, willing Parker to look up at him. "What do you mean 'sign this paper?' I thought I was here to be your wingman." His voice came out harsh and accusing.

Parker flashed him a guilty smile, and Brennen knew this wouldn't be good. "So, it turns out, Meg the matchmaker and I are doing well. Long story short, she burst into a settlement meeting and told me she loved me last week. I was going to tell everyone tomorrow during rowing." He gave Brennen a sheepish grin and, friend or no friend, Brennen was ready to punch him in the face and walk out.

"I can't believe you lied to me." His words came out more of a growl.

Shaking his head, Parker said, "I didn't lie, just didn't explain everything when I was at your house. I knew you wouldn't show if I didn't say I needed your help. Meg will be here in a bit. I'd love to introduce you to her."

"It sounds like you're trying to introduce me to a lot more people than just her." Heat surged up the back of his neck. He didn't need a mirror to know his ears were as red as the dress that girl was wearing. His fight-or-flight response increased as he glanced back at the door not directly in his line of sight. Turning back to Parker, he asked in a flat tone, "Do you need help or not?"

"Yes, but here's the thing. I need you to be one of the daters."

"Are you serious? Me? Speed date?" Brennen pointed to himself, sure Parker had made a mistake.

Parker ran a hand over his face and leaned forward on the table. "Meg always has more girls show up to this thing. She asked me to find a couple of guys to come just in case. Can you just suffer through an hour? Then you can go back to your eerily quiet home. It's not like you're missing much."

"The Red Sox are playing. Or did you forget now that you're in love?" Brennen wished that sounded more degrading than it did. A pang of loneliness hit him straight in the chest as he said it.

Parker pulled out a small ear bud. "Are you kidding? That's what this is for." He held it up to Brennen's ear, and the familiar voices of the radio announcers filtered through his ear. The Sox had just made a double play, ending the inning.

"Well, it's good to see some of your priorities haven't changed." Brennen leaned over and filled out the small form, signing his name at the bottom. "What do I do now?"

"Take this," Parker handed him a 'Hello, my name is' sticker and pointed to the small group of people already inside. "Go mingle with the other daters before we get started."

Pointing to himself, Brennen said, "Did you really just tell me to mingle?"

"I know that's not your strong suit, but it might be good for you." Parker paused before saying, "Just make sure to think before you speak. Some of these people are sensitive."

"Whatever." Closing his eyes, Brennen knew what Parker was implying. Don't be himself. Don't let every thought that ran through his head come tumbling out.

Small talk was boring, and most people thought he was too blunt at first meeting. He didn't like the surface presentation of people. It was probably the reason his dating life struggled. He wanted people to get rid of the façade and be real.

Shaking his head, he walked inside, his stomach tying itself in knots one by painful one. The moment of loneliness had passed, and the logical side of him took over. Why did he need a relationship when his life was near perfect? He had more money than he knew what to do with and plenty to occupy his day. A woman would just mess that up, bringing in her agenda and opinions.

He opted to stand against the wall, hopefully out of sight of the group. He lifted one foot up to steady himself and pulled out his phone. Checking his email, he found several good reviews of the new workout he'd uploaded earlier. Satisfaction floated through him, and his body felt light as a cloud. It was a small victory in what Parker pointed out was his boring life. He just hoped his old excitement for creating the workouts would be there the next time he needed it.

"Okay, daters." Brennen looked up and saw a blond woman standing on a small platform in the far corner.

"Welcome to Speed Dating. I'm Meg Austen, owner of Love, Austen, and we're excited to have you here tonight. I'm sure you're all eager to get started, but if you have questions about anything dating or love related, don't be afraid to ask." A wave of light laughter flowed through the sixty or so guests. If this was who Parker had roped into dating him, he was a lucky guy. She was beautiful and enthusiastic. Better yet, she owned her own business, which he commended. Being self-employed wasn't for the faint of heart.

"We know being here is a big step for some, if not all of you. So, if you don't meet anyone tonight, don't worry. We have a large client pool we're working to match, so you might have better luck there. We have a promo code for the services we offer should you need it."

Sounds like tonight will be a bust.

Not that he was here for himself. He wasn't in the right frame of mind to take on the highs and lows of a relationship, so he shouldn't even have a sliver of hope that his soulmate or true love or whatever would show up. He was just helping Parker, filling one of the male slots.

She smiled at the crowd. "Here are the rules."

Brennen had never been to something like this, but his younger sister Clara had watched enough girly movies to help him get the gist of what tonight was all about. He already felt like a piece of meat as the women stared at him, turning to their friends and whispering. He wasn't a model but with all the workouts and attention to diet, he probably could be. Tonight, though, he wanted nothing more than to relax on his couch, watching baseball.

Everyone shuffled around the room, and Brennen tried to recall the final instructions. Last in line, he didn't have to pick a number from the bucket. Turning, he sat in the last open seat, wishing he'd continued back to his house on the drive over.

CHAPTER 5

Not hearing the conversation between Charlotte and the snooty girl, Lexi kept checking the room, as if her inner magnet pushed her to look for the guy with the hazel eyes and styled light-brown hair.

A guy like that is a heartbreak waiting to happen.

When she spotted him leaning up against a wall, she felt a rush in her stomach, the kind brought on by rollercoasters. Turning away again, she shook her head as if she could mentally get rid of the thoughts trying to invade her mind. He reminded her of her past, one she hadn't bothered to think about for quite some time.

The room filled up, and Lexi was grateful for that. The sooner they got started, the sooner she'd be relaxing at home in her candy-cane-striped pajamas.

Meg stood in front, calling for attention from the crowd. Seeing her there brought a little more comfort. She would always be grateful for the chance Meg had given her to cater the gala a few weeks ago. That bit of advertising was why her truck had been non-stop busy ever since.

After she stated the rules of the night, Meg finished with,

"We're so glad to have you here for this fun event, and we hope you enjoy yourselves. We love hearing how you found out about us or our events, so please leave us a comment card. If someone brought you tonight, or told you about our event, we like to reward those people."

Charlotte poked her in the ribs. "Write my name down. If tonight doesn't work out, maybe they'll give away a free matchmaking package. And I'll give it to you."

"Please, no. Life is going well as it is." Lexi raised her hands as if in defense. "Things are great with the food truck, my sister is engaged, which means I don't have to worry about her relationship woes anymore. I'm in no rush to find someone."

"What you need is someone to help you change your opinion of men." Charlotte gave her a matter-of-fact look, and Lexi's stomach simmered with irritation. Of all people, she'd hoped her best friend would cut her some slack when it came to relationships.

Folding her arms over her chest, Lexi turned with eyebrows raised. She wished she didn't have to tilt her head up to see her friend; it took away from the intimidation factor. "What I need is for everyone to stop playing match-maker in my life."

"Just because Garrett hurt you—"

"I'm not talking about him. Let's just get this night over with already." The rest of the room had already taken their seats, and she was grateful they weren't sitting right next to each other. Charlotte would have needled her for every emotion she'd gone through in the past seven years, as if she hadn't already shared them with her.

She slipped between two tables and sat on the cushioned bench, smoothing out the A-line skirt. Bluntness was her weapon of choice this evening. Most guys wanted to be told how amazing they were for the simplest thing. She wouldn't be indulging that part of their ego.

Meg held out a small bucket to the long line of guys, which Lexi assumed contained the numbers of the table, and a part of her was glad they hadn't somehow been matched already. Not that they could know much from one short questionnaire. She wanted to leave without false promises and regret. Pulling out her phone, she mindlessly swiped and tapped to ease the anxiety drumming inside her. She didn't want to watch as a guy picked her number and sauntered over to her. And he would saunter. She'd already analyzed most of the guys in the room; most of them either believed they were the greatest thing to enter the restaurant that night, or they pretended to be.

A few minutes later, she heard the chair in front of her pull out. She glanced up, giving the small man a smile. He set his hands out on the table, and Lexi shifted a few inches, resting her back more comfortably against the cushion. Taking in his appearance, she bit her bottom lip to keep from laughing as she saw the thick glasses and obvious hair plugs.

Why did she find it so funny? The guy looked sincere. Maybe he just had a hard time finding someone and needed a little boost. She tried to smile as wide as possible, but tension pulled in her neck, and she moved her eyes to examine her fingers.

"Hello, I'm Bob. Real estate agent, dog lover, and all-around carnivore. I'm thirty-five and hoping to settle down with someone amazing." His expression made Lexi's skin crawl.

Settle down?

She might be a dateless wonder, but she wasn't ready for anything long-term, especially after thirty seconds of talking to him.

Straightening her shoulders, she figured she might as well

get some good practice in. Who knew? Maybe one day she'd be able to break her curse of dating. She might as well get out all the awkwardness now.

"I'm Lexi. I'm twenty-eight, a pastry chef and owner of a food truck."

Bob's eyebrows raised, and he scoffed. "You call yourself a chef, and all you own is a food truck? Chefs work in high-end restaurants, right?"

Next.

Heat coursed up Lexi's neck, and she had to roll her lips in to keep from barking at him. She took a few breaths before she said, "Have you eaten at a food truck?"

The man nodded.

"Did you like the food?"

"Yeah, it was pretty good."

"A chef is the head of a restaurant. Even in a food truck, the one cooking the food is the chef. It doesn't have to be a sit-down place to appreciate the work and passion a *chef* puts into their food."

Bob pulled out a toothpick from an ancient leather jacket and stuck it between two of his side teeth, working to free some hidden piece of food. Her eyes grew wide, and she wished she had someone she could silently communicate with, like an eye roll or something. He pulled the toothpick away and asked, "Why not work in a normal restaurant?"

"Do you own your own company, Bob?" The irritation racing through her made her neck itch.

"No. I'm under a broker."

There goes that analogy.

"Never mind. I worked as the pastry chef here," she moved her finger as if to note the whole restaurant, "just a few months ago."

Bob looked up at the ceiling and then the walls, as if

seeing it all for the first time. "You worked here? Did you get fired?"

Seconds passed, and Lexi waited for a bell to ring. Now. And now.

She tried to relax and avoided the question. Could she make this any more awkward? Trying to smile, she asked, "Do you come to these events often?"

He nodded. "This is my third time."

"No luck so far, huh?" *Be nice.*

"No. I went out with a girl a few days after the last one, but she got an emergency call and had to leave. I called her a few times after that, but she's never picked up."

"I wonder why," Lexi said it under her breath and from the expression on his face, he hadn't heard. "Have you tried enrolling in whatever program this company has?" She moved her arms around, trying to signal at the room, as if that affected dating.

Bob shook his head. "No, but I've thought about it. Finding the right girl would just do wonders for my life." His expression softened, and his lower lip quivered.

Guilt. It hit Lexi like the pinch of a needle, the shame seeping throughout her limbs. Not overly painful but just enough to make her feel uncomfortable. She'd been judging this guy when her life was more than similar. This was why she didn't date. It made her irritable and unpleasant.

The bell finally rang.

"Good luck, Bob. I hope you can find someone." She smiled, her first genuine smile of the night. As she watched him change seats, longing for something similar overwhelmed her. The chances of her finding a guy who would understand her work schedule and her family had caused her to push off finding anyone at all. But for the moment, she wanted that more than ever and with how things were going, she wasn't sure that would or could ever happen.

CHAPTER 6

The bell sounding was a welcome relief. The blond girl in front of Brennen hadn't taken a breath in at least two minutes, as if stopping would injure her somehow. He'd nodded his head several times, usually after she said, "Right?" and it was giving him a headache. He'd said all of five words to introduce himself, and his throat was scratchy from disuse. He wished he'd gotten a soda or something from the bar before this thing began.

He shot a glance at Parker, who was talking to the girl who'd welcomed them. The girlfriend. Ugh.

Why couldn't he just skip to that? The stage when they were comfortable enough to state what they wanted without scaring the other person. When they started to discuss a future together.

Dating was rough as it was, and meeting a girl somewhere was one thing. It was another one to have it staged, like an entrée at a restaurant. Main dishes he understood. Women, not so much.

As the next girl began her spiel, he looked down the row and counted the women he'd already "dated" for the night.

Seven. Seven women, and not one had sent a spark of curiosity through him. In fact, he'd only said a handful of words to all of them combined, mostly because they seemed to thrive on a listening ear. As he looked at his third date, he still couldn't believe she'd slid him her phone number before he'd stood to move to the next table.

He glanced back to find his current date crying, twisting a tissue in her hand.

Great. What did I miss? Is she crying because I didn't respond to something? He groaned, wishing he were home watching SportsCenter. Or Food Network, but he couldn't let that get out. His rowing buddies would never let him live it down.

The bell rang, and he moved once more, settling into his chair before looking at his current date. He did a double-take, surprised to find the woman from the registration table earlier. Closer, her eyes were even more captivating, with little golden flecks throughout. His eyes traveled to her lips, wondering if they would be soft. He forced a smile, trying to get his thoughts back on track.

He couldn't help but glance up at her hair, the front reminding him of the ladies in old-time pictures. What was that style called? Bouffant? The rest of her hair was pulled back in a high ponytail, a ribbon matching her dress tied around it. If he hadn't already seen her insane shoes, he would have asked if she were heading to a sock hop.

He focused back on her face, her light-brown eyes boring holes into his.

"Is there something wrong?" she asked, glaring at him. It reminded him of a kid not happy when his mom said no to something.

"No, I just thought your hair was interesting. You look like you hopped out of a 40s magazine."

A coy smile developed on her lips, softening her face. "Does that mean you think I'm a model?" Just as quickly, the lightness disappeared, and a bored expression stretched across her delicate features. She turned to see something at the table next to them.

Funny. Okay, let's try again.

"I'm Brennen Peters. I was born in Chicago, but we moved here when I turned six. My hobbies are rowing and listening to music while I do just about anything." He tried to remember if he'd shared any of those details with his previous dates.

She raised her chin, the corners of her mouth barely turning up. "I'm Lexi Sarmiento. I was born in Boston, and I enjoy good food."

Nothing like both parties being vague. At least they had something in common.

He sat there, waiting for her to start into a tirade, a sob session, or even a gushing fest. She mirrored him, her one eyebrow raised. A thought struck him, and his mouth opened before his brain could stop him.

"Do you..." he began, reaching out his hand, possible questions changing several times before he settled on one. "Do you have a big family?"

He raised his arm up, pulling back the sleeve to see the time. Only twenty minutes until the night was over. He could do that, right? Focusing back on Lexi, he now understood what people meant when they said, "Looks can kill."

She frowned, and it made him smile wider, the pout of her lips drawing him in and surprising him. He dropped his hand onto the table and waited.

"I have one older sister and three younger. The bathroom is sacred at our house. My father had to have another one put in, so we'd stop arguing while getting ready." She laughed, a light, airy sound but not forced. "What about you?"

"Younger sister. She keeps me on my toes."

Lexi leaned forward on the table. "Did you come here on your own? Or did someone make you come?"

"What gives you that impression?" Brennen pursed his lips together and frowned. Leaning forward, he clasped his hands together and waited for her explanation.

"You just seem so excited to be here. And this has been the longest date yet." He caught onto her sarcasm and the withering look she sent to the woman in charge.

He growled, making her head spin. "And I thought I had problems. I guess I could ask you the same question."

"Let me guess. You're a businessman with an ego the size of Texas." She paused, mouth open, to glance up and down at him before continuing, "Or you inherited a lot of money and do nothing in particular every day."

With arms folded across his chest, he said, "I don't call it work. It's more my hobbies that bring in income." Reflecting over the past few days, he'd had his schedule packed with so many things, he had to stop and remember what the date was by noon. But he enjoyed seeing the satisfaction on her face, as if she'd won an internal battle with herself.

The bell rang, and Brennen wasn't ready to move. He hadn't had a good verbal spar in quite some time, and the spike of adrenaline made him smile. She'd made this night well worth coming.

* * *

As the speed dating event came to a close, Brennen stretched, grateful his sixteen dates were over. He leaned over the table, searching for Parker. His friend stood in a corner, talking to a few men and women. Brennen ran a hand through his hair and rolled his eyes. He would pay him back for the conspiracy.

With his eyes sweeping around the room, they stopped

on the girl with the polka dot dress. With a personality as feisty as hers, no wonder it caught him off guard that she was so short. He studied her as she stood next to a tall girl, smiling and laughing, but there was something lacking, like she was holding back.

A hand touched his shoulder, and he looked up to see Parker, a wide grin on his face. "So, any good prospects?"

Exaggerating his eye roll, he glanced back at the poster girl for the jitterbug and shook his head. "Nope."

"Maybe you're being too picky."

"Well, you're one to talk. This is a pot and kettle situation here. Meg is the first girl you've dated in years." Brennen frowned.

"It's a different feeling when you find someone worth a relationship. You're twenty-nine, Brennen. You just need to get out more." The wistfulness in Parker's eyes made him want to gag.

Meg walked over and slid her arms around Parker's waist. She turned to him and smiled. "Hello. Are you Brennen?"

He nodded, trying to smile. "Yep. The friend your boyfriend tricked into coming here tonight." His words dripped with sarcasm, and he was grateful she picked it up.

"Well, these things can't hurt too much. Who knows if you'll click with someone?" She gave a small chuckle, and Parker joined in, only adding to the sappiness of the situation.

Raising his eyebrows, Brennen stared at Meg. "Do you have statistics on the success rate of speed dating?"

She shook her head, giving him a sly smile. "No, but we get a lot of good business after."

Brennen tipped his head back and laughed, harder than he had in a long time. "I hadn't thought of it like that, but that's a good business strategy." He looked around. "Do you need any help cleaning up?"

"I think we'll be good. There isn't too much other than the garbage from the desserts. Did you get something? The gal who makes them does a fantastic job. She just catered the big gala we had a couple of weeks ago." When Brennen shook his head, she said, "Sorry, I've got to help get things wrapped up. It was nice to meet you." She walked over to someone waving to her from across the room. Parker left to help someone move a table, leaving Brennen to stand alone.

"My life is fine. I'm happy the way things are. But thanks for asking," he said to no one in particular. Just then, he saw Rosie the Riveter looking at him, her expression curious, as if she'd heard what he said.

Turning on his heel, he barged through the restaurant and out to the street. His home was calling, and he wasn't about to suffer through any other comments on his single status tonight.

ry as she might, Lexi couldn't pull her eyes away from the one guy she'd glanced at throughout the night. It was easy to make excuses, but he'd seemed like the only semi-normal guy there.

"Hey, girl! How did the night go?" Charlotte's voice pulled Lexi's eyes from the doorway Brennen had gone through.

"Still claiming the Dateless Woman title. But I guess in this case, I had sixteen first dates. How about you?"

Charlotte shrugged. "There were some fun guys. We'll have to see though. Are you ready to go?"

Lexi shook her head. "I need to wait and get my platters. It was nice not to have to set up the entire display this time."

"I bet. All the organizing for this bake-off has been stressful. Sarai will take some extra hours at the truck, right?" Charlotte winked at her, and Lexi groaned.

"I forgot about it. Wait, does it start this week?"

Charlotte frowned. "You just asked me about it last night. Project Fed is like your baby. I can't believe you forgot about it already. Then again, I'm surprised you didn't organize the entire bake-off."

Lexi gave her a courtesy laugh. "It bugged Marla how much I was doing on other events. She thought I was trying to take over her job, so I took a step back. I'm still trying to find a good middle ground when it comes to Project Fed."

"Well, I have a surprise for you."

Lexi's stomach tightened. A surprise in Charlotte's eyes meant she would be assigned to do something uncomfortable. "What?"

Charlotte's hands moved, speeding up to rival the words pouring out of her mouth. "You know you're one of the best bakers ever."

"Right. The best baker wouldn't quit La Crème to open a food truck?" Lexi asked with a wide grin.

Hitting Lexi's shoulder, Charlotte gave a fake frown. "Don't joke like that. You were the top of our baking class. And you're the top baker in Boston." Her face sobered even more as she glanced down at her nails. "I was going to tell you sooner, but I couldn't find a good time to do it. I entered you into the Northeast Baker of the Year contest."

The air flew out of Lexi as if she'd been punched in the gut. "You did not." She paused, hoping her friend would deny it. When Charlotte nodded, she closed her eyes, panic squeezing her lungs. She tried to breathe but felt like she was doing it through a straw. "Why? You know I don't do well in competitions when I'm the actual competitor."

"They sent information to the baking school, and they've changed some guidelines from years past. You'll win for sure this time."

As far as the contest, Lexi wanted to crawl in a hole. Her first attempt at it four years ago hadn't gone well. She attempted it two years later with even worse results. It was like her brain stopped all thought in or out, and she couldn't remember what she was supposed to be doing, wasting the precious time it took to create the intricate pastries and baked goods.

"How have they changed the competition? And why are they starting it so early? I thought they always held the competition during Christmas."

"The gingerbread contest section is still in December, but they wanted to make sure the contestants were more well-rounded. So, the added section is taking part in a charity auction or bake-off."

"But I'm just the mentor in the bake-off. You're not trying to set me up to be in this competition, right?" Lexi's tongue had absorbed all the moisture in her mouth.

Charlotte turned her head a few inches, giving Lexi a look as though she were her mother. "To fulfill the contest, you'll teach someone how to bake several items and depending on how well they do, you get points for the first section of the race."

Throwing her hands up in the air, Lexi groaned. "I can't believe you entered me without talking to me first!"

"You would have said no. I know how long you've wanted it. This is your year."

Lexi folded her arms and pulled them in tight. "And why would they make it so people have to worry about it all year now? It was bad enough when I knew there were only three weeks until the gingerbread showing."

"You'll finish this part of the contest when the bake-off is done. Then you'll have until November to relax or design an elaborate gingerbread creation." Charlotte winked at her, but Lexi searched the room for a trash can, certain she'd be losing the cookie she'd eaten moments ago.

Lexi turned to see Meg walking towards her, several silver platters in her arms.

Perfect timing. She needed a distraction.

"Oh, Lexi. You did it again. Thank you for bringing the desserts for this."

"Yep." Lexi couldn't get her temper to simmer down, and she turned a little to keep from looking at Charlotte.

Charlotte took Meg's hand and shook it. "Thank you for having this event, Miss Austen. It was a fun night."

Meg smiled. "I'm glad to hear it. Did you both participate?"

"Against my will." Lexi groaned. She felt an elbow in the side and gave Charlotte a nasty look.

Laughter broke out, and it surprised Lexi to find it was from Meg. "Girl, I know how that goes. You'll find someone; just be you, and it will happen. I never thought I'd be dating anyone seriously, but the past couple of months have been a whirlwind. You know you can always talk to me about it." She winked and gave Lexi a devilish grin.

"Well, if I were diligently looking for a relationship, after tonight, I'd sign up now. It was rough." Lexi wiped her hand across her forehead, acting like she was swiping at sweat.

"Let me know. You get a discount for bailing me out with the gala." She smiled and then walked away.

Charlotte nudged her. "Tell her you'll use it. Or I will."

Lexi glared at her friend. "I can't right this minute. Someone signed me up for the Northeast Baker of the Year contest." She tried to keep her expression neutral, but the corners of her mouth went up anyway.

"Okay, you're signing up to be matched after the bake-off, or I'm taking your spot. It's time for the Dateless Woman to hang up her cape."

After contemplating the idea for a few seconds, she said, "Deal. Let's go get some food. I'm starving." A few weeks to mentally prepare for even signing up to date would be good for her. By then, maybe she'd have a plan of how to get out of it.

CHAPTER 8

*B*rennen's stomach growled as he thought about food. The morning rowing session he'd just finished with the guys had left him with the inability to focus on anything else but the gnawing in his stomach. He didn't even have to be home to picture what he had there. With nothing but ketchup, pickles, and milk in the fridge, he'd need to venture out to the store at some point.

He laughed as he remembered Parker's reaction to the contents of his fridge. Since he'd never learned to cook, so he might as well not waste money on things he wouldn't eat and then have to clean them out several weeks later. He could stomach a lot of things, but mold wasn't one of them.

Thinking of Parker brought up a mental picture of Lexi. He still couldn't figure out what intrigued him so much about her, but the urge to track down her number and call her for a coffee was more overwhelming by the hour.

He shook his head. That was like playing with a lion. It would only end badly for him.

Pulling out his phone, he opened his note app and clicked on the one with a list of restaurants he kept for review possibilities. The list of breakfast places wasn't as long as restaurants for lunch or dinner, and even though he'd have to fight the Saturday morning crowds, at least it would satisfy his hunger and helping with work at the same time.

His phone rang and he saw Clara's name. "Hey, sis. How's the future nurse?"

She giggled a bit and said, "Doing good. Just took my last final yesterday. I called you last night, but you didn't answer. Is everything all right?"

"Yeah, Parker tricked me into coming to a speed dating thing. It was brutal."

"Great! I owe him twenty bucks now."

A deep growl rose to Brennen's throat. "You bet against me?"

"Just to see which one of us could get you on a blind date first. He definitely wins." She laughed and as much as Brennen wanted to stay mad, he couldn't. Clara was the only other relative he had since his parents' accident, and it was already hard enough having her an hour away at college.

"Yeah, sixteen blind dates to be exact." He cringed just thinking about the night.

"No possibilities? There had to be at least one girl who was somewhat interesting." He could hear the demand in her voice and knew she wouldn't back down until he acknowledged it.

"I barely got a word in edgewise with some of them."

Clara sighed. "Bren, you don't talk much anyway. You were probably content just to sit there and listen."

He nodded and smiled, grateful they weren't on a video call. "There was a girl who was a bit snappy. It was a lively discussion and the fastest five minutes of the night."

"When you say discussion, I assume you mean you argued about something trivial?" That edge to her voice made him wonder who was older.

"More or less. She dresses like she's going to an ice cream shop in the 1940s."

Clara laughed loud and long, pulling Brennen into it. "That's better than what some women wear, especially the ones at those fitness conferences you go to. I always want to throw up when I see a half-dressed woman draping herself over you."

"I didn't know it bugged you. I also never noticed." He thought about the last conference he'd gone to. It had been in Florida, and he felt like all he did was sweat and drink water. When he worked out, it was with tunnel vision of his goals, so he never remembered the women he met at those things.

"Of course, you didn't." Clara spoke, and he could almost picture her expression, wanting her words to be taken seriously. "It's tough to find a girl when you compare all of them to Mom. She had her faults too, Bren. Just remember that."

Closing his eyes, he knew Clara was right. As he did a mental review of each of the women he'd "dated" last night, he'd subconsciously compared each one, whether it was her appearance or how she talked.

"You know me too well." How she knew all she did about relationships after the handful she'd been in caused him to wonder about her. "What about you? Are you dating anyone?"

A pause met his ears, and his defenses went up. "I've gone out with someone the last few weeks, but it's nothing serious just yet."

"Bring him over sometime. I'd like to get to know him." More like he'd rather threaten the man with his life. He'd never felt more like Clara's father than at that moment, something she didn't appreciate being nine years younger and his sister. "Are you heading home now?"

"I've got my car packed up, but I've got to make a stop before I get there. It'll take most of the day. Don't wait on me for dinner. We'll celebrate the end of the year tomorrow. And the fact you're kind of dating."

"Not dating. Playing on my sensitivities to help out a friend isn't dating."

"Whatever, bro. I'll see you tonight."

His stomach rumbled, reminding him of what he'd been doing before Clara called. Closing his eyes, he pointed his forefinger at the list on his phone and tapped. Opening them, he smiled at his random choice. He wouldn't mind trying out their breakfast menu.

The place he chose, Basil, had opened a few months before. He'd had dinner there once, when it first opened, but Brennen had found his readers were interested in not only the opening week, but how service was when things settled down. Besides, he hadn't done a breakfast review in months, living on his protein shakes.

Stepping up to the seating hostess, he raised one finger as she opened her mouth to ask him how many.

"Only one?" she asked, flirtation written all over her.

He nodded and gave her a look to bring her back to the present. Gathering a menu, she motioned for him to follow her through the upscale restaurant to a corner next to a large window. The view of the second-floor restaurant looked out over the back of Boston Common.

Pristine white tablecloths seemed to reflect the chandelier above, and he winced a bit before looking away. The rich woodwork around the windows and doors made it feel like his childhood home, the one he'd known before his parents' accident nine years ago.

"Good morning. I'm Tonya, and I'll be taking care of you. Our Cannoli Stuffed French Toast is the special this morning. Have you had enough time to decide what you want?"

Nodding, Brennen said, "I'll try the special." He looked back down at the menu and said, "I'd also like the breakfast strata, as well as… the cinnamon roll." Closing the menu, he handed it to the girl.

She hesitated before asking, "Are you expecting anyone else?"

"No, but can I get a glass of orange juice to go with the order?" He smiled but felt the force of it. The girl blinked a few more times before nodding and moving out of sight.

Why is everyone questioning my single status all of a sudden? As he thought about his order though, she probably just wanted to know if he would be eating it all himself.

Two tables away sat a couple on the same side of the table, their hands intertwined, leaning over to kiss each other every so often. The vomit sensation rose in his throat, and he turned away, trying to focus on something in the restaurant. When he found he kept glancing back at them, he moved to the other chair, now facing a dark wall. Not the best view, but it would have to do if he wanted to eat in peace.

The waitress' words played on repeat in his mind, her tone on the word 'one' stirring up an unsettling feeling inside him. And as much as he didn't want to admit it, Clara's concerns added to it, like a chorus ringing in his mind.

Maybe Clara was right. Maybe he did need someone to share all this with.

As Tonya placed the food in front of him, his eyes bounced around the several plates, trying to decide where to start. He'd had a good workout this morning, but he would have to up his workouts tomorrow to compensate for all the sugar. As he took a bit of the French toast, he decided the early morning workout was worth it as the creamy texture mixed with the syrup exploding with flavor in his mouth.

It was on days like this he loved his hobbies most of all. Even if he was alone.

CHAPTER 9

A knock sounded at the door to the Sarmiento apartment. Lexi got up from the couch and walked over, opening to find her friend standing there. Dressed in fitted jeans and an orange blouse, her sunglasses stuck into her curly blond hair, she looked more excited than normal. That didn't give any clues to why she'd stopped by.

Waving a newspaper, Charlotte said, "I saw this on my way home and wanted to bring it to you. I didn't have time to read it yet but when I saw 'Roll With It' in the headline, I did a happy dance. I'm sure the guy behind the register thinks I'm crazy."

"You are. But that's why everyone loves you." Lexi smiled and took the paper from her friend. The name of her food truck was written in a box at the top of the paper. Someone had reviewed her truck? She didn't remember anything, so it must have been anonymous.

Pulling pages open to the right section, she sat at the dining table and folded the rest of the newspaper back, scanning for the review. Finding it near the bottom of the page, her stomach sank. Taking in a deep breath, she read aloud.

"The headline says, 'Why we're all afraid to eat at food trucks.'" She lowered the paper a few inches and gave her friend a look before resuming her reading. "'After recommendations from a few friends to branch out of my normal reviews and try the food trucks in town, I started with one called, 'Roll With It.' I was excited about it seeing as the owner picked a 1940s Chevy panel van, a new spin on this food craze and something I haven't seen around. I could look past the fact it's painted pale pink and decorated with cupcakes. What's hard to swallow is the line down the sidewalk.'" Lexi gave Charlotte a look, and her friend cringed.

"'From what I gathered, the truck features a daily special, usually a pastry, cupcake, or muffin. By the time I got to the front of the line and asked for said special pastry, the girl said they were out, and I'd have to come back next Wednesday if I wanted that specific one. I'd already waited in a longer line than I thought feasible for a food truck.' Wednesday. People love the apple strudels. I really need to up the quantities I make for those."

Charlotte nodded. "That's one of my favorites. If you're running out every time, that means there's a demand."

"Don't start with all the economic business talk now. It's too early for that." Lexi scrunched up her face. She lifted her leg onto the chair, still sporting her pajama pants. Sarai was taking over the truck that morning, allowing Lexi the one morning during the week when she could sleep in.

"Fine, but keep reading. It can't be too bad."

Lexi folded the paper in half to make it easier to hold. "'I ordered a cinnamon roll and was disappointed by the lack of frosting. Cinnamon rolls are meant to be covered in frosting, balancing out any dry pieces of roll.'" She skimmed down a few paragraphs and started again. "'This isn't good business. To have a daily special, you shouldn't be running out of the item by three in the afternoon.'" She stopped reading, knowing that it wouldn't get any better from there.

Putting down the newspaper, Lexi's body buzzed with frustration. She'd always apologized to people when she saw a line and tried to get things as fast as possible. And while the article had some good tips, they cut straight to her gut. She'd spent several extra days training Sarai, making sure she knew that customer service was the most important part of the business. From the sound of it, the reviewer had shown up on her shift.

Charlotte took the newspaper and read to herself. After several moments, she said, "How could anyone be that cruel?"

Shifting forward, Lexi laid her head down on the table. It had been hard to give up time at the truck, but she couldn't physically do everything all day, every day. Sarai had done fine with Lexi watching over her shoulder but had the guy just come on a bad day?

"Come on, Lex. You know it's not as bad as this guy made it sound. I've tried every one of your pastries, and I love most of them."

Lexi pointed her finger at her friend. "Most of them being the keywords. Nothing like destructive criticism to jumpstart my day."

Reaching forward, Charlotte took Lexi's hand. "Don't give up now. You've come so far since Garrett and buying the truck. Just go about life tomorrow as if nothing happened. Open the truck, serve your pastries, and smile." She paused, her eyes flitting back to the paper and then to Lexi. "I would think about writing a letter to the Boston World. Some of this article borders on libel. Besides, he sounds like an idiot when he tries to critique your picarones here at the end."

"Don't tell me he didn't like the picarones? I haven't met someone who didn't like them." Lexi looked to the few lines

Charlotte pointed at and sighed. "Who does this Noah Parsons think he is?"

She rested her head on her arms, closing her eyes. She'd felt the increase of pressure after Charlotte's revelation about the baker of the year contest, but now she knew she'd question every action she made in the kitchen for weeks after.

"Let's talk about the bake-off."

Lexi lifted her head enough to give Charlotte a look of hope. "Can I take a rain check?"

Her friend shook her head, a deep crease etched in her forehead. "No. You're not giving up on the competition before you even start."

"Well then, I'm as ready as I can be. We start next Saturday?"

Charlotte's eyebrows pinched together. "Kickoff is Thursday, remember? I need you there that night because the opening and finale will all be taped for that one show, *Everything Your Heart Desires*. They'll air it on Thursday in their regular time slot. Saturday will be the first judging round."

Lexi swiped her hand up to hit Charlotte's shoulder. "Why didn't you tell me we're doing this on camera?"

"What did you expect? We need some way of getting the word out, and taping clips to share on TV each week will help bring in more donations. What are you so afraid of?"

Rubbing her head with her hand, Lexi closed her eyes, trying to block out the current of memories invading her mind. "The cameras make me freeze up."

"What?" Charlotte's expression made her look like she'd just been kicked.

Taking in a deep breath, Lexi was surprised she could finally talk about it. "Anytime a camera is near, I freeze up, overthinking what I should be doing, and my brain goes blank."

"Is that why you turned down being on the CIA ad when

we were graduating? And why you struggled at the Baker of the Year both times? The camera?"

"I'm surprised you didn't know."

Shrugging one shoulder, Charlotte's face hadn't changed. "I just figured with everything happening with your family at the time, well, both times actually, that you just got overwhelmed."

Lexi thought back to the second time she'd gone for Baker of the Year. Her father had gone in for rotator cuff surgery, meaning she had to pick up the slack in the kitchen at her parents' restaurant. When he was cleared to work normal hours again after six months, Lexi had been so exhausted, she'd come down with walking pneumonia and had slept most of the two weeks before the competition.

The first failure happened just after Garrett… She didn't want to go there.

"What has my life turned into?" Lexi moaned.

"Blessings." Charlotte tried to imitate Lexi's mother and left them both in stitches.

It seemed like she just had to get past the next few weeks, get over the rut she could feel herself slipping into, and forge ahead. But what was it exactly that would get her out of that rut?

She thought about the guy from speed dating and for a few seconds, she could have seen herself with him. But then reality set in, her past fears about relationships surged to the surface.

Prepping for the bake-off might help sort that out. Teaching baking was easier than doing it herself. And anything to keep her mind off the dreamy guy with the fiery personality was the surefire way to avoid crying herself to sleep.

CHAPTER 10

*B*rennen stopped at a florist on his way back from the city Thursday afternoon. With a dozen white tulips and a dozen daisies, he set them on the passenger seat. Every now and then, he'd move his hand out to keep them from rolling off as he wove in and out of the streets.

Parking next to Mt. Auburn Cemetery, he turned off the ignition and waited a moment before getting out. Clara had gone out to lunch with friends, and he should've waited for her, but he needed a few moments alone on this of all days.

He trudged up the first hill and walked on the asphalt path for some distance before turning to the right. Weaving in and out of gravestones, he stopped in front of a large stone pillar with a star carved out of the granite.

It looked as though the field had just been mowed, but several longer blades of grass stood up in front of the headstone, not having been trimmed just yet.

Spencer and Caroline Peters.

Brennen took the flowers out of the plastic wrappers and set them in the iron vases on the sides of the headstone. They were both his mother's favorite, and seeing them there filled him with happiness. His dad would've wanted both sides to be for his mother.

It had been nine years since that fateful car crash. Nine years since he'd received that phone call from an unfamiliar voice telling him his parents had died. He'd been at school down in New York and still wasn't sure how he'd managed to arrive home without being in a wreck of his own. How naïve he'd been about the world, thinking only bad things happened to bad people.

His parents had been the best of people, always helping, always serving. If he could resemble a small part of who they were, he'd consider himself carrying on their legacy.

"Hey, Mom, Dad. I've thought about you two a lot lately." He paused, unsure what he wanted to say and not finding the words. Instead, the memory flooded back, as clear as the day it happened.

Arriving at their family home in Belmont and finding a strange car parked in the driveway. It had been a social worker, staying with Clara, trying to soothe her. Days later, he was named guardian to his ten-year-old sister.

Tears streaked down his face now, the cool sensation helping with the May heat. He'd cried many tears sitting in front of their tombstone, but these were different. Instead of remorse for losing such great people and a carefree life for him, he felt the beginnings of peace taking root inside him.

"I haven't done much lately. Fitness Overhaul is second in the app store. I'm sure you guys would be confused if you were here, technology and such." He laughed at his father's frustrations over cell phones before they'd passed. "I went to a speed dating event last weekend. Mom, you'd be proud that I kept my mouth shut when I wanted to set people straight."

"Clara's home for the summer. She just finished her first year of college. Can you believe that? I never thought we'd get to that point." His light tears turned to sobbing, and he was grateful he'd come without his sister. "I'm doing my best to take care of her. I promise. I can't imagine how you felt when I went off to school."

The years of struggle as Brennen had tried to find the balance between parental figure and brother to his sister flooded his mind, a different scene popping up every second. He'd felt like a kid himself at the time and trying to maintain bills and other things had been difficult at first. But they'd stuck together and worked to get to where they both were today.

When his editor's name popped up on Brennen's phone, he scowled and let it go to voicemail. Seconds later, Scott called again. Shaking his head, Brennen picked it up, answering more gruffly than he was used to.

"Hello?"

"Brennen, I've got an urgent assignment for you this time. I think you can handle it." There was a pause, and Scott said, "That last article revision worked out well, by the way."

"Okay. What's the assignment?" If the guy kept calling him this frequently, Brennen wasn't sure he'd keep answering. He'd taken the job for something outside of the routine of fitness, but the demands were getting a little high. And he'd wanted today to be a no-work kind of day.

"The paper is donating a bunch of money to a competition to feed kids in school. I need you to be our representative for the contest." He could hear the demand mixed with hope in his editor's voice.

"What would I have to do?"

Scott grunted and said, "It's a bake-off. For the first taping, you'll need cookies."

"When is the first taping?"

"In about an hour."

Brennen laughed, part of him hoping his boss was joking.

"I might not be a good baker, but I know I can't bake cookies in an hour."

"Just go buy some for this first part. It will make it look even better when you're a decent baker. You can bake a little, right?"

"Define a little."

"Just enough to beat the guy representing the Boston Metro. Do this, and you'll get a bonus." Scott chomped on something, and Brennen had to pull the phone away for a moment.

"What's the name of the charity? Today's the anniversary of something, and I can't really get away right now."

He heard papers ruffling, and he waited, looking at the light hitting the flowers. If he were a photographer, this would be a great shot.

"Project Fed."

Brennen's heart stopped, pulling his gaze away from the flowers. "Are you sure?"

"That's what these papers say."

Taking a breath as he decided what to do, he brought the phone back. "Give the bonus to the event. I want point on the editorial selection this next time. No more giving it to Steve."

"Done. That was easier than I thought. I figured I'd have to do some sort of groveling to get you over there this late. It's at the Boston Baking School." The phone clicked, and Brennen sat still for several more minutes, seeing but not registering anything before him. He had no idea Project Fed was still running. And they'd organized a fundraiser for it?

He glanced over at the headstone again. "As much as I'd rather hang out for the afternoon, I guess I better get going. It sounds like your charity is still helping people. There are people to serve, right, Mom?" No answer greeted him, but a light breeze tickled his face. That would have to do for now.

Walking out of the cemetery, he pulled up his browser

and searched for cookie stores or vendors along the way. The one he'd just reviewed came to mind, but it was too far for one, and he wasn't grabbing cookies from a truck.

A message came through, and he read the address. He'd have to get going if he were going to get there in time. It was out in Chestnut Hill and although that wasn't far from the cemetery, the Boston traffic would be thick at this time of day, on a weekday no less.

By the time he arrived in the parking lot of the school, Brennen had almost convinced himself to leave. He knew nothing about the contest and even less about the actual process of baking. His expertise was in critiquing food, not producing it. But it was for charity and for kids. He'd have to keep telling himself that.

Pulling open the doors, it was difficult to move with dozens of people and camera crews milling about. He'd forgotten to ask if his boss would be there, at least to give him some directions. His eyes scanned the walls for some sign pointing to where he was supposed to be. Someone must have noticed his confusion because he heard a voice come from behind him.

"Can I help you find something?" A blond woman with an earpiece looked at him. She looked vaguely familiar, but his brain wouldn't process at the speed he wanted.

"I'm supposed to be helping with a bake-off? I'm sorry, my boss didn't give me many details." He smiled, trying to calm the anxiety boiling up in him.

She nodded. "Are you the representative from Boston World?" When he nodded, she continued, "Good. You're the last one to arrive. Just follow me over here."

Turning, she walked toward the back wall. The sea of people parted for her, and she smiled and nodded at many, waving to someone at the back of the crowd. When they made it to the wall, she opened a door, and all conversation stopped inside. Brennen bit the side of his cheek, keeping his eyes fixed on things just above people's heads. The disadvantage to working from home meant that he had to psych himself up to talk to people and be himself.

The blonde turned to him and asked, "Sorry, what's your name?"

"Brennen P-Peter-sen." She made a note of it on the clipboard she held. He surprised himself with the small lie, but it was better this way. Being the late founder's son would bring attention he wasn't ready for.

"Hey, everyone, our last contestant is here. We're running behind, so we'll have to do introductions later. Does everyone have your cookies ready?"

Brennen's stomach dropped. He'd forgotten to stop for cookies. As the others filed out of the room, he dashed over to the cupboards, hoping that a baking school would have something already made. Cabinet after cabinet came up empty, and he was sure he would fail even before he started.

Giving up, he walked out of the room and down a hall, trying to catch up with the other contestants.

They passed a conference room with large glass windows. Seeing a small spread on a table, he broke away from the group and searched the table for anything resembling a cookie. At the end of the table, he found a whole tray of them, pink frosting swirling evenly. The only thing telling him they hadn't been made in a factory was the slight discrepancies in the cookies' roundness. Scooping up the whole container and a few napkins, he moved back to join the group, standing behind the last woman.

They'd all placed their cookies on one of the eight carts standing to the side, and Brennen set his down, heart beating wildly at what was to come. Not only that, but he was using someone else's cookies to start off this competition. He'd give Scott an earful about last-minute events after this.

Seven people stood in front of him, four girls and three guys of all heights and sizes. It was too dark in back to see any details of their faces, so he focused on keeping his heart at a steady beat as he stared at the cookies on the cart. If these people had all made those cookies, he wouldn't survive this contest past the first week. His few attempts at cookies had come out more like charred biscuits than soft and edible desserts.

A voice sounded on the platform, welcoming the crowd to the bake-off. Brennen peeked around a curtain and was in awe to see how many people crowded into the large room. He'd walked through a group of people earlier, but now the place was even more packed. Obviously not like a sold-out Celtics game at The Garden, but for a charity bake-off, he was impressed.

Turning his head, he saw the same blond girl who'd directed him before. His brain worked to place her and after several seconds, an image popped up, like an internet search. She'd stood next to that Lexi girl the night of speed dating. This city felt small if he could see someone again that soon.

"We're so excited to see all the support for this bake-off. As most of you know, this competition is benefitting the Project Fed charity started over twelve years ago here in Boston. We'd like to show you a clip of what your money will go toward."

She stepped back, and the lights went dim, a large picture flashing onto a white drop mat. Music played, and a picture of some kids at a table smiled back at him. It shifted to several other pictures, all emphasizing the process of the meals and the happy kids. A male voiceover spoke as the pictures kept scrolling.

"Project Fed has helped over twenty thousand kids in the Boston area in the past five years alone. Founded by Caroline Peters after noticing the need for good meals for the kids of the city, Project Fed began as an organization out of a storage shed and has since grown to what it is today."

The screen switched, and a man with graying sideburns spoke, his title as CEO of the charity written below his face. "We want to keep Caroline's original vision. She would always say, 'A full stomach opens the path for a fed mind.' We work to make sure kids of all ages are getting the food they need to concentrate on their studies. I know how cranky I get when I haven't eaten, and some kids go a few days without more than scraps. And when school is out for holidays or the summer? It's even worse. No kid hungry is a goal we can accomplish together."

The video ended, and the lights turned back on. The girl, Charlotte, resumed her position on stage.

"This year, we wanted to add a little fun to our fundraiser, and we came up with the idea to have a bake-off. We've put a lot of work into this, and we're grateful to the TV crews and journalists joining us to help spread this great cause. Let's start by announcing the contestants."

Brennen's mind went into overdrive, and he wondered whether he should just slip out now. The crowd was large, and he wasn't sure how this would go. He didn't mind parties when he could be almost anonymous, but when the attention would be focused on him… It made him want to throw up.

"Brennen Petersen? Are you still here?" Shaking his head, Brennen moved onto the stage, pasting on a smile and waving to the crowd. There were a few cheers here and there, easing his discomfort a notch.

Charlotte spoke again. "We're grateful for their willingness to participate today. Now for how this will play out. I've only discussed this with our professional bakers, and I'm hoping you're all as excited as we are. We have eight contestants to match up to our eight pro bakers, which we'll do in just a few minutes. We'll have a theme each week until we're left with the final two contestants. The final challenge will determine the winner of the trip to Jamaica, graciously donated by Boston Travel & Cruise located over in Brighton. Any money raised by media and other avenues over the course of the competition will be given directly to Project Fed."

The crowd cheered, and Brennen looked down the line, recognizing a few faces among them. One city councilman, a news anchor, and others from around the city. A competitive feeling swept over him, and he faced forward with his chin high. He could pay for a trip to Jamaica on his own, but he wanted to win this, to prove he could figure out how to bake. It was something new, something exciting, and it would break up the boredom he'd been feeling the past few days with his routine. Not to mention the it was a matter of pride. He'd spent the last nine years not realizing his mother's charity was still running, and winning the competition would help make up for that in part.

Someone came and ushered them off stage, telling them to hurry and get their plates ready for the eight judges. Charlotte's voice echoed in the background, something about extra questions and how the crowd could donate to the cause. Brennen's mind was so focused on what to do with the cookies, most of it didn't register.

The girl next to him pulled cookies out of a plastic container and arranged them onto small glass plates, all set on a large silver cookie sheet. She looked over to him as he pulled out the napkins and arranged the stolen cookies.

"That's what you brought? Store-bought sugar cookies?" She raised her eyebrow.

"I just found out I was supposed to be here. This was the best I could do."

She smirked. "Well, at least you won't last long then. I need that trip. My husband and I haven't been on a trip in four years, ever since our kids were born." Brennen wasn't sure what to say to that, so he nodded.

A woman called out to them, dressed in similar baking apparel to what Charlotte had on, and Brennen assumed she was Charlotte's assistant. They gathered together, the woman holding her clipboard out in front. "Okay, bakers. This is the line-up for presenting to the pro bakers. A couple of us stagehands will serve your cookies to them, and they will ring a bell if they want to be your coach. If there's two or more, you'll get to pick who you want to work with."

Dread filled him. As she went through the list, he was set to go last once again.

Longer to wait, and longer to let the humiliation set in from his lack of skills. He needed to learn to say no in the future.

exi couldn't catch a break. She'd rung the bell for the cookie that had practically melted in her mouth with flavor. But four other pros had tapped in, and she lost to the one with the most accolades. She'd tried for another three of the cookies, her expectations dropping with each one. Each time, she'd had to debate why the contestant should pick her as a coach and every time, she lost the battle.

Now, on the last choice, she wondered why they bothered to bring out the cookies for everyone at all. This person would be her student, and she prayed it would be someone competent.

Charlotte had told her they'd made sure the contestants didn't have any culinary experience, which meant they could learn from the pros and still make the competition exciting. Lexi wasn't sure she could handle a total newbie.

The staff wheeled out the carts, just like they had for the past seven, placing a napkin with a cookie in front of each pro baker. The others had nice plates or even decorative paper plates, but this one had opted for napkins.

Great. She wanted to slide under the table. The review

article she'd seen a few days before spun on repeat through her mind. She would get the cookie reject, the one who would need all the extra classes to catch up with the rest of the group.

As the cookie was put in front of her, her jaw dropped open. She looked up at the rest of the table, and a few eyes turned to her in confusion. In front of her sat the pink swirl sugar cookies she'd brought to the back room to share with the rest of the judges.

Jordan Lancing leaned over and said, "Is this a joke? These are yours, aren't they?"

"Yep," Lexi said, popping the p. She caught Charlotte's eye and narrowed her own as she reached out and tapped the bell in front of her.

She had to help someone who brought her own cookies to the bake-off. Was that supposed to be flattering?

Charlotte faked the fanfare that had come with choosing the other contestants. When Lexi turned around, she stopped, frozen in place. This had to be some practical joke. There stood that Brennen guy from the other night and when he looked at her, his eyes flew open, his face drained of color.

"Thank you all for coming," Charlotte said to the crowd. "We now have our teams. This week, and by that, I mean two days from now, we'll be having our first competition, making rolls. We wish you all good luck. If you want to come by and watch the bake-off, we'll get started at one in the afternoon. Donate in the boxes near the exits of the school, or you can go online to projectfed.com and click on the donate tab. We'll keep an up-to-date count of donations as we try to meet the goal of twenty-five thousand. Thank you all and good night!"

The crowd clapped and cheered. Lexi sat still, her eyes unfocused as her brain registered everything that had taken place in the past five minutes. She'd have to spend the next eight weeks with the jerk from speed dating. Who had also tried to pass off her cookies as his own? What were the odds?

She finally stood and walked over to him, annoyed that she felt so short now in her flats. Her head barely hit his shoulders.

"This is a surprise," she said, clasping her hands in front of her.

"Likewise. Did you miss me?" Brennen's eyes twinkled.

"Not even a bit. Seems like we've been cursed." The look on his face told her he felt the same. "So, where d'you buy your cookies?"

He frowned, his eyebrows pinching together. "I didn't—I mean, I wanted—I got a call an hour ago that I was supposed to be here. I didn't have time to make anything."

He looked sincere, and Lexi didn't want to torture him anymore. She'd have enough time over the next few weeks.

"Points for honesty now that it's just you and me. I thought you told me your name was Brennen Peters." She looked at him and blinked lazily, trying to convey the fact she could wait all day for an answer.

He shook his head. "Um… I must not have said it, um, loud enough for you the other night." Putting his arms out to his sides, he asked, "So, what do we do from here? We have to make rolls or something?" Brennen shifted his weight, stuffing one hand into his dark denim pants pocket.

"Good question. We figure out a time to practice and then we get here early on Saturday to make them. Let's see," she said, looking at her watch. "It's five now. Can you meet tomorrow evening?"

"Friday night?"

Lexi set her hands on her hips, bugged she had to tip her head back to look up at him. As much as heels killed her feet and calves, there were certain advantages to them.

"Yes, Friday night. Do you have plans or something?" A worry shot through her that he had a date. Not that she was interested in him at all. But that jawline and his gorgeous hazel eyes made her regret the tone.

Project Fed. We're doing this for the kids, not so you can check out some jerk.

He seemed to study her reaction because after a few seconds, he said, "No. I'm just surprised you didn't come away with a date at the speed dating thing."

Lexi scoffed and scrunched her nose. "You were the best-looking guy there. Too bad your attitude needs an adjustment."

A coy smile made her want to smack him. "So, you think I'm attractive?"

What is this, middle school? Then again, she'd said something to that effect at La Crème.

"Can you meet tomorrow or not, Casanova? I've got to be somewhere soon, and I can't be waiting for you all night."

"Yeah, I can meet. Do we practice here?"

Lexi nodded. "It's the best place for it. Charlotte said the classrooms on the east side of the school should be open after six tomorrow. Rolls take a while so come on time and prepare to stay late."

"Can I put your number in my phone?"

Lexi hesitated, unsure what to do. She'd never had a guy ask her that. "You missed your chance to date me, buddy."

Brennen gave her a strange look and burst out laughing. "You thought I wanted to ask you out? Not going to happen. I just figured if I'm running late or if you forgot to pick up some ingredient at the store, it might be beneficial to have your number."

Heat rushed to Lexi's face and she closed her eyes. Of course, he wasn't hitting on her. She rattled off her phone number and resisted the urge to check the message he'd sent so she'd have his. Why did she feel so off around him?

"Perfect. I'll see you tomorrow here at six sharp. And I wouldn't wear such nice clothes if I were you. Wouldn't want them to get ruined with flour and dough."

Turning on her heel, she walked off the stage, not wanting to converse with him more than she had to. Her cheeks still burned at his laughter about the phone number, and she wanted to avoid him at all costs. Of all the people she'd been assigned to, why did it have to be him? She'd have to be on her guard every moment she spent with him.

This would be a long competition. Could she hold on long enough to qualify for Baker of the Year?

CHAPTER 12

The whole event had rattled him, and Brennen didn't know whether to be sick or to laugh about the whole thing. He sat behind his steering wheel, staring at his reflection in the rearview mirror. His first conversation with Lexi at speed dating replayed through his mind. She'd said she liked good food but hadn't said anything about being a professional baker. Not that knowing that could change much now.

He shifted the car into gear and smiled as he thought of her feistiness. It was as though the spices she used for baking were part of her personality. He liked that she spoke her mind, as it was refreshing for a woman to get straight to the point. And that she didn't try to turn on the charm every time he saw her added points in her favor.

But he'd lied about his last name and real connection to Project Fed's founder. From the way she'd looked as he admitted his white lie about the cookies, if he ever had to admit that he was Caroline Peters' son to her, it wouldn't go over well. The challenge in her eyes had been enough for him to stick to the lie.

He merged onto Beacon Street, heading toward home. Traffic was still heavy at nearly eight in the evening. He did everything he could to get past it but no matter which lane he chose, it seemed like the other would speed up, causing him to make no progress at all.

His thoughts turned to his parents and to the charity. His mother had started Project Fed his senior year of high school after volunteering at Clara's school cafeteria for the previous year. Even in their more affluent neighborhood, there were several kids without the means of having lunch, and sometimes even breakfast.

He remembered one night as she poured over several books and resources from the internet, finding the statistics of kids who went without lunch and how many of those only ate every so often. She'd been the driving force to change that in Boston, her hopes that it would carry on to all of Massachusetts, and even further west if possible.

Rubbing at an ache in his chest, the guilt ate at him that he'd forgotten about the charity. But for so many months after the accident, Brennen had done everything he could to keep his head above water. Dealing with grief, being thrust into parenthood, and trying to figure out what he wanted to be now that the chance to be a normal college kid had been taken away. At least others had kept it going in her stead.

As he made it home an hour later, he walked in slowly, still waist-deep in memories.

"Hey. You're home late. What happened?"

He looked up to see Clara, her hand on her hip, reminding him of Lexi. Seeing the girl twice, and he was already comparing? He pushed the thoughts from his mind and said, "Scott called, and I'm now part of a bake-off."

"You bake? Is this something I've missed since I went to college this last semester? Because last Christmas didn't have any of these baking skills filling the house with cinnamon and cloves." She smirked at him, her hands waving around the room. The expression made him laugh harder than he'd meant. Just thirty seconds with Clara home, and it already felt less empty, something he was grateful for.

The last time he'd tried to bake was when she was turning sixteen, and he wanted to make her a homemade cake, just like their mom would've done. But he'd forgotten about it in the oven and ended up having to throw the pan out because it had turned to charcoal.

"Um, nope. I showed up and didn't have the cookies I was supposed to have for the professional bakers. So, I snuck some from the side table, and it feels a little like I cheated." He walked toward her, and they moved into the kitchen, where several takeout boxes awaited them.

"I'd say that's definitely cheating. What are the pro bakers for?" She took a seat at the bar and resumed eating the Chinese food on her plate.

Brennen ate a piece of broccoli before responding. "We're paired up with one. I guess they teach us how to bake or something, and then we have to do the weekly challenge on our own? I'm still not completely sure."

"Well, if Scott is behind it, I'm sure you didn't get the full details. When are you going to quit the paper? You're making plenty with the app, right?" Clara stared at him, her fork poised in the air as she awaited his answer.

"It's something different, and it's a good excuse to eat out so often."

"You mean an excuse to eat alone at a restaurant."

Brennen shook his head. "That's not it, but it's a bonus. When it gets boring, I'll be done with it. But as scary as this bake-off sounds, it's a little exciting. Maybe I can learn a few things, and we can put this kitchen back into use. Then again, we'd probably have to clean off a layer of dust in the oven before we used it." He made a face, and Clara burst out laughing.

"Yeah, we don't need the fire department over here for an actual fire this time." They both laughed, and Brennen realized it felt good to laugh with her, filling the house with noise.

Clara took a bite of food, chewing slowly. Once she'd swallowed, she asked, "Is there a charity they're doing this for? Or is it just some publicity stunt for TV?"

The questions caught Brennen as he placed a large piece of beef in his mouth, the meat getting stuck in his throat. He pounded on his chest twice, and the piece dislodged, allowing him to breathe again. He stood, retrieving a cup and filling it with water. After a sip, he said, "The bake-off is for Project Fed." He kept his back to her, not ready to see her reaction.

"It's still going?" The emotion in her voice caused him to turn, seeing the bottom of her eyelids had filled with water and at any moment, the dam would break, sending several drops cascading down her face. Brennen stared at them for a moment before he nodded.

"From the slideshow they shared, they've helped over twenty-thousand kids. Mom would love knowing that." He let the moment lie and slid back onto his seat next to Clara. Ready to steer the conversation to safer topics, he asked, "So, have you made any summer plans?"

Clara coughed a couple of times and pulled a glass of water to her lips. Brennen patted her back, trying not to laugh at how awkward she was suddenly.

When she regained her composure, she glanced over at him, her expression sheepish. "Well, I applied to be a camp counselor down in Pennsylvania. I leave a week from Monday."

All the excitement he'd felt at having her home dissipated.

"When were you going to tell me?"

"Tonight. Hence my peace offering with the Chinese food." She waved at the white boxes as if he should've known. In a way, she was right. When was the last time she'd bought food? "My original intent was to make food since I got home earlier than expected. But it looks like you're going on a starvation diet of some kind."

Avoiding the light jab, Brennen focused on the fact she was leaving again. "How long have you known?" He turned toward her, sadness and betrayal moving through his chest.

She shrugged, her fork drawing designs through her rice. "A couple weeks. I knew you'd be upset that I applied at all. But it will be good to have this on my resume. I'll be an assistant to the nurse as well as a counselor some weeks."

"Are you sure you don't want to just bum around here for the summer?" Loneliness wrapped itself around him again, intensifying the feelings he'd had over the past few days. This big house had been quiet for so long with her gone to school, and now she was leaving him again.

"I can't do that forever, Bren. And I know you've basically been my parent for half my life, but you don't need to worry about me anymore. I'll be fine."

He shook his head. "I'll always worry about you. You're my sister. I just don't want you to go through another situation like you did with Kyle Whiteman."

Reflecting to the summer before brought back a flood of memories, still a sour pill in his stomach. Clara had met Kyle Whiteman at a party, and they had hit it off, from her side anyway. She'd fallen for him, but it had taken some time for Brennen to convince her that Kyle was only there for money. When he found some evidence, Kyle ran, leaving Clara with a broken heart.

"I'm being careful. I promise. This is such a great opportunity to get some experience. With all the activities at a camp, I'll be a pro at first aid." She winked at him, and he felt resigned to a summer of boredom. At least the bake-off was something out of the ordinary.

"What about the guy you said you were dating?" Brennen asked, trying to be nonchalant.

Clara's mouth twisted, her tell that she was trying to hold back tears. "He had another girlfriend. So, we're done. That's why I really want to go to this camp. I just need a break, you know? I feel like with last year and now this guy, I just need to go somewhere I don't need to worry about guys."

Brennen put his arm around her shoulder and pulled her to him in an awkward hug. "You'll find someone soon enough, sis. I'm rooting for another ten years, but he'll come along."

She sat back and sniffed. "Thanks, Bren. Find someone while I'm gone. You need a woman to keep you in line, and I need a sister." She gave him a quick laugh and went back to eating her food.

He turned her words over in his mind. He hadn't thought about it from her perspective before, but he liked that. They could grow their little family and for a second, he got lost in that fantasy. But then the reality of it came crashing down, and he knew it would take a lot more than a couple of dates throughout the summer to find the one he could spend forever with.

"I'll try, Clara. But I promise nothing."

The brightness of her face made it hard to know she'd been close to tears moments before. "As long as you have some dating updates by the time I get back, I'll take that as a win."

He blew out a breath. Clara always knew how to tug him in directions he didn't want to go. It all depended on if he was ready for the change or not.

CHAPTER 13

He was late. Lexi calculated times in her head, knowing that with each passing minute, they'd be here even later that night. Mixing the dough, letting it rise, forming the dough into rolls and then letting it rise before cooking. She folded her arms and tapped her foot. It was the courtesy of respecting other people's time. The least he could have done was send her a text. That was one of the reasons he'd asked for her number the day before, right?

She undid the straps to her apron and retied them tighter, smoothing out the mint and brown fabric. Her ponytail had come loose, and she pulled it out, twisting the elastic around her long hair for a messy bun this time. She'd decided on a blue polka dot headband this morning, and she straightened it, glancing back out to the parking lot at the same time.

Checking her phone again, she debated going to the room and getting started. But then she remembered this was for him and not for her own practice. Just as she was about to turn and go, she saw a sleek black car pull into the parking lot. She watched as Brennen stepped out of it, his t-shirt pulling against his pectoral muscles.

When he got closer, she realized she was standing next to the door like her mother at curfew. She moved a few steps away and pretended to pick up some garbage on the floor.

The door opened, and he must have seen her because he said, "Sorry I'm late. Did you get my text? Some idiot double parked down the street over here, and I couldn't get past."

Just as he spoke, her text notification sounded. She forgot that service at the baking school was limited. Holding the phone up, she waved it back and forth a few times. "I just got it." Guilt. Humility. She'd jumped to conclusions, and he'd tried to let her know.

"Where are we going?" Brennen pointed in both directions and waited for her to signal to him.

"We're in a classroom over here." Lexi pointed to her left and walked a few steps ahead until she reached the room. Once inside, she pointed to one of the baking stations, prepped with a mixer, measuring spoons, and a large tin of flour.

Looking around the room, Brennen's face held a quizzical expression.

"What?" Lexi asked, leaning her hip against the counter.

"Everything's so white. All the walls, the cabinets, the floors."

Lexi laughed. "Yeah, that's how Charlotte's parents liked it. They gave her control of the place a couple of years ago, and she's working on some upgrades. Color is one they definitely need here."

She motioned for him to stand next to her. "Okay, how much baking experience do you have?"

Brennen gave her a fake smile, which looked more terrified than anything. "Um, not much. I tried to make a cake for my sister three years ago and got a visit from the fire department."

Lexi took in a deep breath. This would be a long night.

"I should've figured, what with the perfectly frosted cookies that look like the ones at that food truck, 'Roll With It.'" She turned to find he'd stiffened like a board. Giving him a strange look, she pulled some of the tools closer and said, "That means we're starting at the very beginning. So, we'll start getting the dough ready and from there, we can go over the tools of baking."

"Why do I need to know about the tools? Don't you just tell me how to make the recipe, and that's what I do tomorrow?" She couldn't tell if he was challenging her or just not excited about the whole process.

"There will be a quiz during these events." She paused long enough to gauge his reaction and was rewarded with panic etched into the fine features around his eyes. "Okay, so not really a quiz but a game of questions. If I were you, I'd want to look as knowledgeable as I can because every time you earn money, your sponsor matches the amount."

"The newspaper?"

Lexi nodded. "Actually, you've received several other sponsors in the past twelve hours. So, the better you bake and the longer you stay in the competition, the more money these companies will donate to the overall cause."

She smiled as the information sank in. Of all the ten places she'd contacted, eight had already responded saying they'd love to contribute. She'd have to make sure Charlotte added the information in social media posts and anytime they were promoting the event, but every bit helped the kids. A nice tax break never hurt the companies involved either.

"Since we have to wait for the rolls to rise anyway, this will be a quick crash course to get you up to speed."

He pinched his lips into a thin line, and Lexi turned, not wanting to come off creepy as she admired his chin. He drove her crazy, but there was still some pull toward him that frustrated her.

"Okay, so with rolls, we need to start with yeast, warm water, and a bit of sugar."

"Why sugar?"

Going into teaching mode, Lexi looked at him, hoping to make it clear and keep her voice void of irritation.

"Sugar helps the yeast become more active, so it will help with the rising process. Here are the ingredients. Go ahead and measure them according to the directions here." She leaned over his arm to point at the card she'd created for him. A whiff of his cologne hit her nose, and she looked up through her lashes to his face. Wow, he smelled good. It wasn't a scent she could put her finger on, but it was manly, not something she was used to living in a house of five girls.

She stepped back, smoothing the side of her hair as she mentally told her heart to put on the brakes. Brennen moved forward and mumbled the directions of the recipe while his pointer finger scanned the words.

"What does a capital T mean?"

And just like that, she was back to reality. She had a job to do, and that wasn't to stare at him like he was some ancient Peruvian god. He needed to at least learn the basics so he could survive more than one week in the bake-off. There was no way they could cover everything he needed to know the first night. Maybe she wouldn't be stuck with him for too long.

"Tablespoon. It means tablespoon. And 'tsp' means teaspoon."

He nodded, picking up the measuring spoons and checking the recipe again. At least he wasn't guessing. She'd have to threaten him if he did that. Baking had to be precise. Throwing ingredients in at random quantities usually meant a failed bake.

Her phone sounded, and Lexi swiped to answer before realizing it was her mom calling.

"Lexi, where are you? You're supposed to be here for a date with Aaron."

"Please tell me you didn't drag that boy back to the restaurant?"

"Alexis, that's enough. I know what you need, and it's a man. Come home now."

What I need is for people to leave me alone! She needed to find an apartment or some space where her mother couldn't monitor her comings and goings so easily. The hardest part was spending money for a place she only had time to sleep at.

Groaning, Lexi took a minute to steel herself for the onslaught to come. "I can't, Ma. I'm teaching someone how to bake for the contest tomorrow. Besides, did you realize that Aaron is way too young for me? Please, just let me figure out my own love life. Ceila can supply you with grandbabies soon enough. I've got to go."

Hanging up the phone, Lexi closed her eyes. She pinched the bridge of her nose, trying to center the wild emotions running through her. When she turned and saw Brennen with a smirk on his face, she wished she could melt into the floor. The conversation had been too personal to have in front of him, and her cheeks burned as she realized how the conversation might have sounded from his spot in front of the mixer.

"I'm sorry about that. My mother is, um, crazy."

"Sounds like she's trying to get you married off."

Lexi scowled at him, not liking the joking tone. But as she thought about it, it was better to vent to this near stranger who wouldn't be in her life for more than a couple more days, pending his results in the competition tomorrow. "Yep. Her latest victim is six years younger than me. Is it too much to ask to not push when it comes to relationships?"

He shook his head. "No, I know how you feel. But I wish

the push were coming from my mother instead of my younger sister."

"Why not your mom?" She could feel the air shift around her, the tension growing.

"She and my father died in an accident a few years ago." His words came out in little more than a whisper, his eyes focused on the beater as it broke through the thickening dough.

Lexi put her hand over her mouth. "I'm so, so sorry. I didn't know." All the harsh things she'd said and thought about him now tinged with the newfound information.

He gave her a small smile, a sentiment of regret laced through his next words. "It's all right. Just remember you love your mom."

She tried to think of something to say, but nothing sounded as profound as she'd hoped. She could bake some of the most intricate pastries and breads, but talking to human beings was a constant trip down memory lane of awkwardness. And now she felt even worse for how bugged she'd been with her mom, especially since he'd lost his.

"No luck for you in dating either?"

He shook his head. "No, not yet. But I like my life the way it is, and I don't know why everyone's always trying to change it."

With those words, Lexi found herself unable to come up with a response. It was so like how she'd been feeling that she hoped it was honesty coming from him and not an attempt to appease her.

"At least you're not alone there. I'm thinking I need to create a sign that says, 'I'm single, and I like it.'" She laughed as she said it, knowing her mother would probably destroy the sign the first time she hung it.

"You could always make one that says, 'Don't ask me about my relationships.' Something to get the point across."

The corner of Brennen's mouth turned up, and Lexi felt a warmth flood her chest. The barbs along the walls she'd constructed seemed to dull, and she was more curious than ever about the man who stood before her.

Lexi turned off the mixer and lowered the bowl, the ball of dough ready for the proofer. "It's quite refreshing to hear a guy feel the same way. I just thought that was how my family was since Charlotte's parents haven't put any pressure on her in the dating department. If anyone, she worries about it too much herself."

"My sister Clara is a lot like that. She jumps into relationships like a kid jumping into the pool, with everything she's got and no worries about drowning."

"I have a sister like that as well." She looked at him, surprised that despite their background, they had so much in common.

The next three hours flew as they covered and recovered the information about basic baking practices, all while waiting for the dough to rise. They talked trivial things but nothing as substantial as relationships. But when everything was cleaned up, a part of her was sad the night was over.

Brennen was the first guy who didn't force her to meet some cookie-cutter design for the perfect girlfriend. And that scared her most of all.

Breathe. Just breathe.

Brennen stood behind his baking station and tried to focus as Charlotte outlined the rules of the day. He'd worked with Lexi until one in the morning the night before since he'd forgotten to add the yeast to the dough the first time while she was on the phone with her mom. She'd watched him like a hawk after that.

Five o'clock in the morning came early, and he'd been tempted to sleep in instead of rowing with the guys. But after a few moments of sleep deliberation, he'd decided to get his workout over for the day. He'd just have to sleep in tomorrow.

Lexi had done her best to be patient, taking deep breaths every few minutes as if to calm herself before hurting him. He'd been able to get under her skin a few times, taking away some unease hitting him at being so out of his element. Learning all of this gave him a big appreciation for all the time his mother spent making desserts and goodies when he was growing up.

"Okay, bakers, you have three and a half hours to finish

your rolls. Ready, set, roll!" Charlotte smiled at the crowd, and Brennen felt his limbs fill with lead as he tried to hurry things along. He'd have to get the dough done and put in the proofreader, or whatever they called the little container in the station. Proofer. That's what Lexi had called it several times. Then he'd have some time in between to keep his thoughts from self-defeat and his attractive pro baker.

Her abrasive personality was growing on him. Not enough for him to consider a future with her but enough to feel a smidge more comfortable in her presence. She was nothing like his mother, and he was grateful he had someone he could compare girls to, hoping to avoid a trip to Parker's divorce law firm... ever.

After their conversations the night before, the similarities between them were more than he could have imagined, and he found himself amazed over and over again at the depth to Lexi's character. But he'd have to think about that when he wasn't on the clock.

The pro bakers sat in a line at the front of the room, and Brennen avoided glancing up at his coach, unsure if she could read his mind at this point. His mixer was kneading the dough at a high rate of speed, and he wondered what he would do while it rose. Raised? Since when did he worry so much about grammar?

"You'll want to get that in the proofer as soon as possible. Mine's already been in for a few minutes." Brennen turned to see that baker from the other night, Jessica Pace, at the station next to him. She sat on a chair, looking bored.

She said it to get under his skin, but he wasn't in the mood for it. He had to make sure all the possible outcomes for failure didn't happen to him today.

Since when do you care about this? Since the moment he'd heard the words 'Project Fed.' Since it would help kids in a worse position than he'd ever been in. It was giving back at its purest form, and he'd do his best to give them that opportunity. At least for his mother's sake. Besides, with a suddenly empty house for the summer, he had to have something to fill his time besides workouts and columns.

He worked the dough after it had risen the first time, shaping it how Lexi had instructed him. Several of the pieces didn't stay rolled up, but he didn't have time to waste as they had to rise one more time. And he'd already lost enough seconds and minutes with his slow, unsure movements.

Back in the proofer, Brennen wondered why anyone would be crazy enough to bake. There was so much time in between, and his brain decided it was the perfect time to show him every memory of his shortcomings. Boredom had a funny way of doing that.

By the time the rolls were out of the oven, he had thirty seconds to brush butter over the tops and put them on actual plates this time.

"Time's up, bakers. Hands off your station." Charlotte looked around and made sure everyone had stopped working.

Brennen took a step back, staring at his rolls, amazed they looked edible. Their forms weren't all a tight circle, but they looked done, the buttery brown top glistening and making his mouth water.

Brennen brought his plates up to the front table, where two judges would decide who was the Week 1 winner and who would be going home. From the look of all the rolls, he was around middle of the pack, which made him feel more comfortable.

Charlotte stood before them. "Congratulations, bakers, on making it through your first challenge. Let's get the judges out here so they can give us their thoughts on your creations."

A man and a woman walked through the door at the back.

Walking along the table lined with the various roll creations, they talked and made comments about each of the rolls and as much as he strained to hear, they talked too softly to glean much. By the time the talking was all over, Brennen's stomach was in his throat.

The judges left to confer, and Brennen sank down onto his stool behind his station.

"How does it feel to have the first challenge over?" Lexi asked, putting the rest of the rolls on a plate.

"I'll let you know when I can breathe. It's not over until they tell us who's done and who wins."

Lexi waved it away as if that wasn't a big worry. "You'll be safe for this week at least. Table three over there burnt hers." Brennen tried to laugh quietly, and Lexi wore a smug expression before turning serious again. "We just need to focus on whatever next week's theme is. One week at a time. If you're on social media, share that you're part of the competition and how to donate. And you work for the newspaper. Any plugs you can give us will help. The more presence you have, the better your chances for contributions."

"I can do that." Lexi took a seat behind his station, and he sat next to her, watching the door for the emergence of the judges.

The room was nearly quiet, as some of the audience whispered about this thing or that. The cameras had moved around, filming everyone during the baking portion, and he was sure they'd be back for the first announcement.

Five long minutes later, the man and woman walked back into the room, and Lexi walked back to her seat next to the wall with some of the other pro bakers. "Sylvia, John. Have you made your decisions?" Charlotte asked.

The two of them nodded, and Charlotte smiled. "Perfect. We'll have you hold that thought for just another minute or two." She had to pause for the number of groans rippling through the room. Brennen chuckled. It was almost like a commercial right at the most suspenseful part of a movie. "We have a few questions here and for each right answer, our sponsors will donate one hundred dollars to Project Fed. A correct answer will give you five extra minutes in the next bake. Are we ready to roll?"

They couldn't have done this during all the wait times? Thinking about it some more, he was grateful they hadn't interrupted him. He might have ended up with the burnt roll.

"Which of the following types of flour has the highest starch content? Is it A) Cake flour, B) Bread Flour, C) All-Purpose Flour, or D) Pastry flour?"

Flour? They'd worked on the baking tools and other vocabulary, but nothing like this. He turned to scowl at Lexi, and she just shrugged, holding her hands out to the side.

A few hands shot up, and the guy named Troy said cake flour was the answer. He was right.

"One last question for today's show before we let the judges reveal their decision. The following Italian cookie is known for being twice-baked. A) Amaretti, B) Bruttiboni, C) Pizelle, or D) Biscotti?"

The brunette in the first row raised her hand and guessed biscotti. With another right answer on the first try, he looked at Lexi again, giving her a goofy grin. She covered her mouth as her body shook. From the look in her eyes, he could tell she was laughing, and it sent a thrill through him.

"Our head baker today is Jessica Pace. Congrats, Jessica," John said. The small crowd who'd shown up clapped, and Brennen tried to be optimistic. So he wasn't first this week, but he was determined to be there by the end of the competition. It would take a miracle and a lot of training from Lexi, but that meant he'd be able spend more time with her. His stomach clenched as the next announcement was made.

"As for the baker who falls below the red line, we're sorry

to say that you will be at home for next week's competition, Stockton McCloy. Your rolls overrose and ended up falling flat. Thank you so much for being here and taking part in the bake-off. Good luck!"

Stockton waved to everyone and left through the back door. Brennen turned his attention to the girl who'd burnt her roll, smiling like she'd snuck a cookie without someone noticing. He'd probably feel the same way in her spot.

Charlotte wasn't done. "Okay, everyone. This next week we'll be practicing and perfecting our biscuits. Good luck, and we'll see you back here next Saturday, same time."

Everyone clapped and moved to clean up.

"Can you meet for practice on Monday?" Lexi said behind him.

He shrugged. "Yeah, that should be fine. What time?"

"I'm off at seven, so after that. We just have a lot to cover for the next challenge."

"Okay, I'll meet you here. It won't take as long as the rolls, will it?"

Lexi studied his face before she answered. "No. Biscuits are faster. But we'll need to review more information, so you don't look like a deer in the headlights when the trivia questions are asked." She laughed, a deep guttural sound, and Brennen joined in.

"I didn't look that bad, did I?" Brennen asked, trying to catch his breath. Lexi tried to imitate it, only sending them into another fit of laughter.

Lexi looked at her phone and saw the time. "I'm sorry, I've got to run. Have a good weekend, and I'll see you Monday." She turned to walk away, and Brennen watched, her graceful movements surprising him. The fact she'd been able to laugh so freely drew her to him more, and feelings he'd thought were long and buried when it came to women surged through his chest. He turned away, willing his thoughts to think about something, anything else.

He wasn't quite healed from his last betrayal, no matter how well he was getting along with Lexi Sarmiento. He wouldn't survive another heartbreak.

CHAPTER 15

He was already ten minutes late, and she was about ready to give him a tongue lashing. After a long day at the food truck, she wasn't in the mood to stay there teaching him all night again.

As Brennen walked in the door, she saw the anger in his eyes, which only sparked her fury more. It wasn't her fault they'd been paired up. She had to get him to at least the final three if she wanted any points toward her baker of the year honor. Since when she started caring about it, Lexi wasn't sure. It drove her crazy she had to work with someone else, someone who didn't value her time enough to arrive when they'd agreed.

They'd made significant progress to be amicable when they'd been practicing and at the competition, but Lexi felt like she was back at square one. If he didn't value her time, she'd walk out and forget the bake-off and the competition altogether.

"Nice of you to show," she said, hoping her fake smile would give him a hint to how she felt.

"Don't. It's been a long day, and I don't want to be here."

Lexi stretched up to her full height, still several inches shorter than Brennen. With her hand on her hip, she set her jaw and narrowed her eyes. "I've got news for you, *chamaco.* This isn't the first place I want to be either, but there are kids out there in need of meals, and this is the best way to raise the money for it. I've had a long day too, but I'm here, trying to make it so you don't look like an idiot in front of a bazillion people in Boston for the next challenge."

He glared at her, looking like he was ready to bark. But he kept his mouth shut, and Lexi was grateful for that as her fury still raged.

"Also, this is the second time you've been late, and we've only practiced twice. If you don't respect my time, I won't respect yours. Lexi's first rule of baking is to arrive early, at least ten minutes or so. There's always plenty to get prepared before baking can begin, and I won't be doing it for you anymore. The later you get here, the later we'll stay until you've got the technique mastered, understand?"

His eyes locked with hers, and Lexi felt her resolve weakening some. The intensity of the blue with the green specks caused her mind to go blank. When he said, "Yes," she had to think back to what she'd asked.

Turning to the table, she focused on the job at hand, pointing to the bowls and ingredients she'd already prepared. "Okay, let's get started."

BRENNEN POURED the ingredients into the food processor, trying to do things fast to make up for the time he'd been late. Her comments were on a loop in his head, and he winced every time she got to the part about him disrespecting her. He prided himself on being early to everything, but it seemed he hadn't made this whole process his top priority.

When all the ingredients were in the processor, he turned it on pulse, watching as a clumpy dough formed. They hadn't spoken since he'd started the recipe, and he could feel the tension building.

"What made you want to become a pastry chef?" he asked, ready to wave the white flag. He leaned against the baking station, awaiting her answer. Lexi handed him a carton of buttermilk and pointed to the directions in front of him.

She shrugged, wiping up some flour on the counter next to the processor. "I grew up in a restaurant and while it was an okay job for most of my life, I like desserts and pastries more. It's like art; I can create different designs or looks to normal things. Whereas with just cooking, you can't play around with it as much."

Rinsing out the cloth, she placed it neatly over the faucet and stood on tiptoe to see into the food processor. She'd relaxed a bit since he'd walked in, and that attraction zipped through his chest again.

"What is it you do again?" she asked, turning her brown eyes to him.

"I'm a journalist at the Boston World and the creator of Fitness Overhaul, the fitness app."

Her jaw dropped open. "You're the guy who owns Fitness Overhaul? I never would have guessed it."

He feigned hurt, and she smiled. "Why not?"

"I just figured it would be some guy hopped up on steroids who had to turn sideways to get through doors. You seem relatively normal compared to the fitness people I've met." They both laughed at that, and the same airiness from their five-minute date floated through the space between them. He liked it. The way her eyes danced at the same time made him laugh even more.

"No steroids here, and I'd like to think I'm normal. I'm not invited to any celebrity parties or anything, so I think that's safe to say."

"My sisters have used your app. Does it take a lot of time to record the workouts?" Curiosity flowed from her, and he grinned.

Shaking his head, he said, "Most of the moves have already been recorded. We did a lot of that back when the app was being created. The nice thing about that is I can just plug the moves into the workout I release each week. I guess the hardest part is coming up with the right sequence of moves and lifts."

"How do you balance that and the newspaper? Do you know that Noah guy?" A scowl darkened her features as she spat the name out.

"Noah Parsons? The food critic? Yeah, you could say I know him pretty well."

Where was this conversation going? Her expression had changed quickly with the mention of Noah. He tried to think if he'd done a critique of where she worked, realizing she'd never told him the name of the place she baked for. Making a mental note, he answered her question.

"Being a journalist has been an adventure. My editor gives me jobs in all sorts of areas, but it's easy to work on both. I'd probably be bored without the writing aspect."

Lexi turned to look back at the bowl and pointed for him to turn it off. "What has been your favorite?"

"I don't think I really have one. I've done some food critiques, and those have been nice. It's easy to like your job when you get to write about food."

"Did Noah take your position on the restaurant reviews then?"

What is her fascination with Noah? His mind spun, not ready to reveal to anyone that Noah was his alter ego.

"Yeah," was all he could think to say. Wanting her to return to the more agreeable Lexi, he pointed to the concoction in the bowl. "So, what are we making?"

She whacked his arm with the back of her hand, shaking her head. "Biscuits, of course. Did you forget in the last two days?"

"We couldn't just buy the ones from the can at the store?" He gave her a crooked grin, and she balled up her fist and punched him in the arm, harder than before. For someone who grew up with only sisters, she knew how to hit.

"No, we cannot buy some biscuits from the store. Those are awful. Have you ever had a homemade biscuit?"

Brennen shook his head. "It's been awhile."

"Well, we'll have some ready for the oven soon, and then you can savor the flavors of the fluffy deliciousness." Her eyes closed, and her nose wrinkled as the smile grew wide.

When the dough was ready, she instructed him to roll it out on the counter. He tried to match her smooth rolling skills, moving the rolling pin in different directions, but it seemed like he'd made no progress.

"No, you've got to apply force to get the dough to roll out, like this." She reached over his arms and put her hands on top of his at the ends of the rolling pin. With the height difference, she had to lean to the side to see the dough.

For a girl who worked with her hands, it surprised him how silky her skin was. Soft electricity pulsed through him, not the kind that shocked but something soothing. She pushed their hands forward, and he could feel the effort she put in. "Sometimes, when the dough bounces back, I hold it in place with the rolling pin to get it to stay."

Brennen saw as she did it, and how the dough seemed pinned in place to the counter. She let go of the pin, and he felt the absence, that tension gone. The movement caused her scent to waft up to him, the smell of spring flowers.

"Now, let's cut them out and get them ready to bake. We want them to be nice and fluffy." She handed him a small, round metal piece. "Just make sure you go through the dough and twist a little. It makes it easier to remove from the rest of the dough."

He cut one in the corner of the dough and then placed the ring down at another point several inches away. Just before he went to push down, she stopped him.

"No, no, no, no. You want to get the ring as close to the other one, so you don't have to roll out the dough over and over again. Have you never made sugar cookies before?" She locked eyes with him and then said, "Oh, wait. You have from your selection cookies. How long did those take to make?"

"I, um. I never thought of it like that." He averted his eyes and set the ring up next to the last one he'd cut out. When she didn't make a sound, he pressed down and twisted. After pulling back his hand, he saw a perfect circle sitting there. Lexi picked it up and slid it onto a baking sheet.

Waving her hand at him, she said, "Keep going. They're no good to us raw."

"You're kind of demanding, you know that?" Brennen said, one eyebrow cocked.

She beamed at him. "You won't remember or learn how to do it if I do all the work. I'm the motivation here, so get cutting."

Thirteen minutes later, the biscuits came out of the oven, filling the room with a scent he'd forgotten. Biscuits had been one thing his mother baked most, and he pulled in a deep breath, hoping to push back the tide of tears threatening to break down his cheeks.

Lexi left the room and came back with some butter and a tub of strawberry jam, the homemade kind. Tears pricked his eyes as he tasted the jam. The perfect topping to the perfect biscuit.

"What do you think?" Lexi asked.

Brennen turned away, trying to avoid her gaze while getting a napkin. He didn't need her asking any more questions than she already had that day.

When he'd composed himself, he turned back to her, throwing the last bite into his mouth. "They were great. I can't believe I didn't burn them."

She wagged a finger at him and said, "You better not burn them Saturday. You're leading the group with donations."

He frowned, confused. "What do you mean, I'm leading the group?"

"You haven't heard? You've raised the most money so far."

"But I didn't get head baker last week." His confusion turned to teasing as he wiggled his eyebrows and smiled. "Must be my charming good looks helping others to donate to the cause."

"Oh, please. Don't get such a big head. We've only done one challenge so far. Don't go thinking you're the best thing since whipped butter."

"I haven't heard that one before. Pastry chef joke?"

Lexi rolled her eyes and shook her head. "Sure, if you want it to be. Just make sure you focus on the process and not the competition. There are kids who need those meals to survive day to day."

"You're pretty passionate about it. Do you have experience with the charity?"

"Not in receiving it, no. We never went without food, even when the family restaurant was just getting started. But I've been working with Project Fed for the past four years, and they are near and dear to my heart. It's amazing the transformation of grades alone when kids have a full stomach."

He didn't know what he'd expected to hear from her, but the fact that she was so passionate about something his mother started made him smile. This girl had a lot of layers to her, and he was more curious than he'd ever been about a woman. But then again, it could have been nostalgia melting his defenses.

Was she worth the risk to let them down completely?

CHAPTER 16

Things had seemed too easy, and she should have known it wouldn't be. Teaching Brennen to bake was like teaching someone how to walk after an accident, painful and slow. But at least he was good company, and he'd showed up ten minutes early to every practice they'd had after she exploded.

It seemed like the moment this contest had begun, no, the moment Charlotte had told her about this being a part of her score for Baker of the Year, Lexi hadn't been able to think straight. The award had been something she'd wanted ever since graduating culinary school, but after the two miserable attempts, she hadn't even thought a win would be possible. But now they'd made it onto week two, causing her hopes to raise another level to up the chances of success for the award.

Here they were, the day of the competition for the biscuits, and Lexi just prayed she'd gone over everything with Brennen. She hadn't heard what kind of biscuits they'd have to make, and so she'd gone over all the ones she could think of. When she instructed Brennen to make cheddar biscuits or drop biscuits or even ones with dried berries in them, he'd looked at her like she was crazy.

"Why would you ruin good biscuits by putting all this stuff in them?" His hands had been flying, accentuating his words, and she couldn't help but smile at the memory.

"People do that all the time. I thought you'd done some restaurant reviews. You haven't seen anything like this before?"

"No, I'm not good with the breads and desserts. I can explain, in detail, all about meat and potatoes, or other main entrees, but breads and desserts are lost on me."

"Let's just hope you haven't said anything about those things in your reviews. Nothing like an ignorant man to ruffle a few feathers about something he doesn't understand." She couldn't help but think of that jerk who'd reviewed her truck in the paper. That Brennen knew him made her want to get the introduction so she could give the ignorant jerk a piece of her mind.

"Are you ready?" she asked him now, waiting a few minutes before the official start of the challenge.

He smiled, but it didn't cover his face like normal. When she'd told him about the amount of donations coming in being highest from his link, it had thrown him for a loop. Right now, he looked about as confident as she did anytime she was on camera.

"Ready as I can be. Let's just hope they don't ask for the berry biscuits. I still haven't had success with those." No, he hadn't. They'd been doughy in the middle every time, despite all her instructions. But he'd tried so hard, and she'd seen a competitiveness come out in him, like he had to win this competition at all costs.

She placed her hands on his shoulders and smiled at him, waiting until he looked her in the eyes. With the height difference, it felt like she was getting ready to hug him.

"You can do this. Just work through it and do the best you can. Keep your eye on the clock and work through the recipe. Kids will benefit from this, no matter if you're a good baker or not." They stood there for several moments, the tension charged between them, and it took several seconds for her to step back and regroup.

Charlotte stood and welcomed them back for the second week. Looking around, it surprised Lexi to see so many people still showing up to watch the proceedings. When her friend spoke again, Lexi shifted forward in her seat, crossing her fingers they didn't want the berry biscuits either.

"We know all you bakers have been hard at work this week, perfecting your biscuit recipes, and we're excited for the results. Especially the film crew." Charlotte paused as loud laughter rippled through the crowd. When they quieted, she said, "You'll be making two kinds of biscuits. One with dried berries and the other will be drop biscuits. You'll have ninety minutes from now. Go!"

"Really?" Brennen whined at Charlotte.

Lexi rested her head against the back of her chair, knowing ninety minutes would seem like the longest span of her life.

She watched as Brennen read through the recipe in front of him, pulling out several ingredients from his shelves below the baking station. He was handsome bent over like that, his face twisted in concentration, even if she could only see his profile. She wasn't sure if there was a rule about not dating her mentee but with everything she'd learned about him, he was growing on her more than she cared to admit.

Would she survive opening herself up to love again? She wasn't sure she wanted to find out.

CHAPTER 17

Ninety minutes to finish two sets of biscuits. Were these people insane?

Lexi's soothing words just moments before echoed in his head. It was for the kids, after all.

Brennen did his best to measure out the flour, as well as the other dry ingredients, dumping them into the food processor. Holding the carton of buttermilk over the bowl, he poured in a bit at a time, making sure he wasn't oversaturating it. With some melted butter and cheddar cheese, he hoped to have some variety to put him above the other contestants.

The show's crew had taken away all timers for this challenge, and Brennen didn't realize how dependent he'd become with something so small. After getting that batch on a pan and in the oven, he made a mental note of the time on the oven clock.

Rushing to wash his tools, he then worked on another batch of dough. These were much harder to roll out with the berries inside but with the clock ticking away, he had to focus and get them done. As he waited for the first pan to cook, the adrenaline had worn off, and exhaustion hit him. If he'd known better, it was as if he'd just done three of his workouts back to back.

Opening the oven door, the cheese biscuits had turned into a pile of melted cheese with a few pieces of breading inside. His stomach sank. He'd forgotten how much cheese Lexi had said worked for the biscuits. Pulling them out, he slid the tray with the cranberry biscuits in to bake. He didn't have time to make another batch of drop biscuits. Running a hand through his hair, he tried to avoid eye contact with Lexi, knowing he'd only see disappointment there.

He'd been so sure of doing well with the drop biscuits because they were easier and faster. The confidence he had in the other biscuits would have him done with the competition for good.

By the time the other biscuits cooked, his mind had conjured up all the awful possibilities. He opened the door to see the tops of the cranberry biscuits lightly browned, breathing a sigh of relief. Picking one up, the bottom boasted almost the same color. They just needed another minute or two, and he hoped it would be enough to keep him in the bake-off for another week.

Looking up, he saw Lexi sitting up in a hard chair, looking out around the room. She wore the red polka dot scarf in her hair again, the one she'd worn the night of speed dating. A strange tickle moved across his chest, feeling like the fizz of a soda. He was surprised to find something so simple could look so striking in her black hair. He wondered what it would be like to run his fingers through it as the curls at the end of the ponytail looked so soft.

He'd been so focused on finding someone like his mom, who could balance out his stubbornness, his pride at being the best at everything, that maybe he'd overthought what a relationship was all about. He and Lexi were so similar in those respects, but it was the little things that caused him to want to text or call her several times a day, or just be by her.

Why am I thinking about us that way? We haven't even been on a date yet. Yet? Ugh.

Then again, these practice times had felt like they'd slowly been getting to know each other. In a way, it felt like speed dating had been a blind date, and they'd just been on a date every couple of days. The amount of talking and sharing had increased each time, and Lexi was probably the most interesting woman he'd ever met.

He looked down at the time and pulled open the door. Charlotte's voice counted down the seconds as Brennen used the oven mitts to place the biscuits on the plates. Looking at the finished product, he had half a chance at continuing his stay in the competition and an equal chance at going back to fitness workouts and newspaper columns. It surprised him how much he hoped he'd still be here.

"That's time! Bring your plates up front, and we'll bring out the judges. This week's judging will be blind."

His heartbeat thundered in his ears, and he stepped back from the table. This time, they were told to stand in a line a foot or two from the judging table. He stood next to the six other bakers, the most nervous he'd been since being here. There were several people who'd come to watch the whole thing and even though he didn't recognize anyone, he hoped he wouldn't screw up. He'd been fine so far because the attention wasn't just on him. He'd have to worry about that more if he made it to the finals.

Sylvia and John appeared, smiling at the contestants and taking a seat behind the dishes. Starting with the first plates, the judges raved over the first of Jessica's biscuits. He kept his eyes forward so he wouldn't scowl at the woman. He had to hold back a smile when they spoke of the rubbery texture of the other.

The judges progressed through the rest of the biscuits and made comments here and there. There weren't many-decent looking ones, and one plate looked more like oatmeal than a biscuit. When they arrived at his plate, he braced himself for the worst.

"This is quite the plate, right, John? First, we have a puddle of cheese and then we have a beautiful cranberry biscuit. The top and bottom look lovely," she said, breaking the biscuit in two, "and the middle is fully cooked." She handed part of it to her judging partner, and they tasted it, causing him to hold his breath.

"Delicious biscuit. I'm not going to attempt a taste at the other," John said. "It looks like too much butter and cheese took over the dough of the drop biscuit here."

After the last plates had been tried, the judges left the room for a bit and returned no less than ten minutes later.

"Judges, have you made your decision?" Charlotte asked.

Brennen had never hated suspense more than at that moment. Stopping for commercials was one thing, but to take forever to make a decision on the baking only caused a throb to begin in his forehead.

"Yes, we have. This week's head baker is... a tie. It seems two types of biscuits tripped up most of you but this one," Sylvia said, pointing to Jessica's plate, "and that one over there are the winners of today." Brennen's mouth dropped open as he registered the plate the judge pointed to. He turned to Lexi, her eyes wide, and her face brightened all around. Wow, she was beautiful.

He turned back and nodded to the judges, ready to announce the person who would be kicked off. Brennen didn't hear who it was, still on cloud nine that he'd won something. Clara wouldn't believe it.

Jessica scowled at him, but he shrugged. At this point, he felt like he'd won the lottery, and he didn't mind sharing part of it with her. All with a cranberry biscuit.

The cameras left the room, and Brennen was happy this week was only about highlights for the local television shows. That meant he wouldn't have to stick around for the boring interviews they needed to cut in. He turned, still stunned about winning, and found Lexi walking up to him. She wrapped her arms around his neck and drew him in, giving him a hug like he'd just won a state championship.

"Congrats! That's awesome. See what all your hard work did this week?" Lexi raised her eyebrows as if that would help emphasize it all.

"Yes, but I couldn't have done it without your teaching."

"Okay, true. At least you see that." She winked and then turned, her expression sober. "We still have a long way to go before the final. We'll meet Monday again to go over quiches."

Brennen chuckled. "Lexi the machine. That's what we should call you."

A slight smile caused his stomach to flip. "What do you mean?"

"You've got your eye on the prize. I can respect that. But first, did you see that the berry biscuit actually worked for once?" He picked her up and swung her around, the two of them laughing loudly.

When he set her down, it seemed like every eye was on them, some people whispering. Brennen brushed it off. He'd been so sure he was going home, to still be in the competition felt amazing.

"I've got to run back to work," Lexi said, checking her phone. "But meet here again on Monday." She grinned at him before turning to walk away.

Arriving back at the house two hours later, after clean-up and traffic, Brennen was surprised to find the elation of tying for head backer hadn't left.

"Why are you so happy?" Clara said, looking up at him from the couch.

"I was head baker this week for the biscuits." He dropped

his bag on the floor and sank next to her, grateful for the comfortable cushions after the day of standing and worrying about his performance.

"Wow. Did you pay off the judges?"

Brennen frowned at her, leaning over and poking her in the side. She doubled over, and he poked the other side, alternating back and forth every so often until she cried out for him to stop.

"That's for thinking I can't bake."

"You don't remember trying to make something on the stove and having it warp the pan because you left it for so long? Your baking skills are as bad as your cooking skills."

Shaking his head, Brennen said, "Lexi is a good teacher. I think that helps the most."

"Lexi, huh? Are you two getting close?" Clara winked, and Brennen pushed her shoulder as he shifted back to his cushion.

"No, we're just practicing the bakes. Other than that, she probably thinks I'm ornery."

Clara put her hands down on the couch and leaned closer to him, staring into his eyes. "Shape up then, big brother. You need to be nice, show you care, or that you aren't all ice and steel like you want everyone to believe."

"Ice and steel? I'm not that bad, am I?"

"When you're in a crowd of people, you tighten up like a zipper to a pair of pants. Loosen up, have fun and be the goofy Brennen I know is in there."

"Dad wasn't goofy." Brennen focused on the TV screen, trying to figure out what his sister was even watching.

Clara put her hand on his arm. "You've got to realize that Mom and Dad weren't perfect. Make your own life and nurture your own relationship. Find someone you can click with rather than someone who's just like Mom."

"I just want to make sure it will work. No use in wasting

each other's time dating for years when I can move on to find someone."

"You can't get to know someone unless you hang out more than once." Clara's eyebrow raised and with her lips pursed like that, she looked exactly like their mother when she'd been angry at him for one thing or another.

Ready to change the subject, he leaned his head back on the cushion. "Are you all packed for camp?" Even this topic made him uncomfortable, but it was the best way to diffuse some of the irritation he felt at the trending topic of relationships. She was heading out again in two days. He didn't want to push her away every time she came home for a break.

"Almost. I've got my last load of laundry in the dryer right now. I'll be heading down there tomorrow morning so I can get settled in before the campers arrive Monday."

"You're leaving a day early? I thought we'd go hit up our favorite spots tomorrow before you head out."

She gave him a sympathetic look and patted his cheek with her hand. "I'll have two weeks at the end of summer before I go back to college. We'll do all those things then." She wasn't asking. And it hurt. All the elation he'd felt at sharing head baker dissipated.

Brennen stood and left the room with a quick good night. Shutting his door, he lay back on the bed and stared at the ceiling.

He was twenty-nine and yet, he still felt like the twenty-year-old college student who'd received a call that his parents had died in a car accident. Maybe what he needed was the assurance it was okay to date now. Clara was old enough to take care of herself.

Who am I kidding? I'm still not ready for a relationship.

Moving on with his life was one thing, but in which direction and with whom were questions he didn't have answers for just yet.

CHAPTER 19

*L*exi breathed a sigh of relief once Brennen made it through quiche week only because one of the other contestants burnt his quiche to a crisp. She was surprised they made it through cracker week at the middle of the pack the week before, seeing as how every one of their practice sessions had ended with nearly chipping a tooth on the rock-solid pieces.

Brennen had been fun but distant, as if there was a lot weighing on his mind. If she weren't careful, she'd be hoping for a relationship by the end of the competition. But every time they were together, she forgot about being careful and enjoyed every minute. She just wished there would be a reason to go on a date that didn't involve practicing baking skills.

She arrived at the baking school thirty minutes early as usual, walking over to inspect a new set of tools Charlotte had just bought. When she came out, she saw a man squatted down talking to a young boy. Lexi recognized the boy as being one of the teacher's sons, and as she took a few steps forward, she recognized Brennen with a ball in hand.

Brennen stood up and told the boy to run. With only so much room in the front lobby, the boy took off, and Brennen threw it, the ball sailing through the air and then in and out of the boy's arms.

"Oh! So close, Mason. Grab the ball, and let's try again."

Lexi ducked behind a pillar, not sure what she'd say if he caught her watching him. She'd never seen him so carefree and, well, happy as he was at that moment. When Mason made it back to Brennen, she heard him say, "Keep your eyes open the whole time. You've got it on this run."

The boy took off again and this time kept the ball tucked up against his chest. With a look of delight, he ran back to Brennen and gave him a high five.

"Ow! Mason, you've got some strength there, buddy. Let me see your muscles." Mason moved his arm to a ninety-degree angle and flexed. Brennen pretended to squeeze the muscle and said, "Wow! You're pretty strong."

The boy grinned, and Brennen handed him back the ball. "Okay, I've got to get to the room and set up before my teacher comes. Will you be here again on Wednesday?" Mason nodded, and Brennen gave him the thumb's up, moving in the direction of the classroom.

Lexi leaned against the pillar and stared at the wall, trying to calm her heart. She felt that pull towards him even more, as if a few more strings had been affixed between the two of them. But then again, she was his mentor. If he'd felt something, she was sure he'd have said something by now. And just a couple of weeks ago, he'd said he wasn't ready for a relationship. Why, she still wasn't sure, but she needed to find out soon before she got too attached.

Mason moved out of sight, and Lexi walked to the classroom they'd been working in for the past few weeks. She'd seen improvement in Brennen's promptness, but she hadn't realized he'd get here this early. Did he do it often? And he'd been so sweet to Mason, which made her rethink her hatred of all things relationship. Garrett had never been one for playing with kids, no matter how big. As much as he'd hurt her when he left, she'd always wanted to have kids, and if they'd gotten married, she probably wouldn't have achieved that dream.

Walking in the door, she pulled her apron out from the cabinet and tied it around her. Brennen strolled out from the pantry and smiled at her.

"You're here early," she said, pulling the bow tight around her waist. "What time did you get here?"

"Oh, not long ago. I was in the neighborhood, so I figured I'd come over since our lesson was soon. How's your day been?" With those beautiful eyes and handsome smile pointed in her direction, Lexi had to reach out and hold onto the counter just to stay upright. She stared for longer than she should have and turned her heard, trying to think of the answer to his question.

Lexi pictured the red-faced lady who'd come to the food truck a few hours before. She'd been angry that the croissants had sold out just before she'd arrived. "I've had better days, but then again, there have been worse ones. Should we get started on our tarts?"

He nodded and stood next to her at the island, his scent wafting over to her. She inhaled and tried to compose herself, willing her mind to focus on the instructions she needed to give him. Why was she attracted to him all of a sudden?

Well, if she was being honest, the attraction had grown over a hundred different facial expressions and peeling back a few layers to the vulnerable part of him. It was insane to think a month ago, she'd been ready to take his face off with the slightest comment, and now she wanted to stand next to him, talk to him, laugh with him forever.

She gave him the first few directions. He nodded and set to work without complaint.

"What? No resistance?" Her smile was close lipped, and he laughed.

"I thought I'd try a new approach to just doing what you say. I didn't on week three and almost lost out of the competition. Then we made some progress last week when I kind of listened to you. I figure if I'm compliant, we'll breeze through the rest of the competition." He smiled wide enough to flash his bright white teeth, and Lexi wasn't sure she'd make it all the way through this lesson with how her body swooned every two seconds.

She liked how he said, "we." Lexi felt the heat surge to her cheeks and laughed, hoping to cover it. "Did you just compliment me?"

Brennen stopped and looked at her, his hazel eyes staring through her. "Yeah, I think I did. Don't get too used to it." He gave her a lopsided grin and went back to measuring the ingredients for the short crust.

Breathe, Lexi. Breathe. One compliment doesn't mean he's in love with you.

She was turning into the over-analyzer she'd been back when she worried about dating and boys. Back when things with Garrett felt off. No wonder she only ever had one date with each guy since.

"How did you get into creating a fitness app?" she asked, trying not to look him up and down, even though he looked good in a fitted tee and jeans. It was the most casual she'd seen him until now, and she was convinced he looked good in anything.

"When my parents passed away, I came home from school to take care of my sister."

"I almost forgot you have a sister. How old is she?"

He shrugged. "She's nineteen and studying to be a nurse."

He paused for a moment and then continued, "I was studying business management, something my father thought would be good for me since I didn't know what to do with my life. After they passed, I got into a routine where I would study and workout, study and workout. I was curious about fitness and diet, trying to figure out different results for certain techniques."

He looked to her for approval to pour in the next few ingredients, and she nodded for him to continue. "My roommate at the time, Jorge, is brilliant with coding and all the technical stuff. He worked through the backend work while I came up with the routines and workouts. I just bought him out about six months ago, and he's started his own company for making apps. I have him do the maintenance on Fitness Overhaul still. I wouldn't trust it to anyone else."

"Wow. I never would have guessed all that. Impressive." She nodded her head and looked down at his handiwork with the crust, rolling it out smooth.

"You have a bunch of sisters, right? I remember you saying something about needing a new bathroom."

Lexi tipped her head back and laughed. "Do I have to claim them? I have an older sister and three younger sisters. I think we're at all points of the crazy spectrum, but they're family. That's why I put up with so much."

"Like your mom trying to set you up."

Why did he have to remember that?

"Yup, like my mom trying to set me up at the same event where my sister got engaged. Or my younger sisters and their lineup of boyfriends."

"You don't have the same?"

Lexi gave him a look to see if he was crazy and then rolled her eyes. "No, dating isn't my forte. Sometimes I wish I could just fast forward to the part when I'm in a relationship and go from there. The whole dance of 'Does he like me?' or

'Is this how I'm supposed to act?' is so exhausting. I just want people to be real. Because if they aren't, I get a little sarcastic, and then things go out the window."

"You? Sarcastic? Never." He grinned, and she slugged him in the arm. His solid, muscly arm. Focus, focus. "You've really never had a boyfriend?"

Lexi paused for a moment, trying to decide if she was ready to talk about Garrett.

"I had a boyfriend for about three years. We broke up around the time I quit law school and went the culinary route instead."

He seemed to consider her words before asking, "What happened?"

"I found out he'd been dating some other girl for that last year. He'd graduated with a bachelor's the year before me and had a career already. I was always studying random court cases, trying not to fail the next exam or paper. I guess I just got too busy for him. But once I found out, I was done. I hate it when people lie. That's a cop out for not wanting to feel uncomfortable telling the truth."

His face hardened for a moment and then relaxed into a neutral, somber position. "Yeah, cheating doesn't make for a strong relationship."

"And you? Is there a parade of broken hearts you've left behind?" Lexi was surprised how much she wanted to know about his past relationships. In all their lessons, they hadn't come back to their dating history.

Brennen tossed a piece of leftover dough up in the air a few times. "I was thinking about this a few days ago. I haven't dated much since my parents' accident. I think it was because I had Clara to protect, to guide, and to raise. With school and trying to keep our parents' house, working to figure out what to do with my life, I think dating just wasn't high on my list of things to get done."

"And now?"

He blew out a breath. "I'm warming up to the idea. I guess I'm just a slow learner."

"Aren't we all? Let's get this in the oven, and we can make the pastry cream."

Her surprise at his lack of dating life made her wonder what really held him back. Someone with that face, with that incredible jawline, and those lips, it was hard to believe he didn't have girls fawning all over him. The thought of it made her jealous. She'd have to avoid his lips from now on. Looking at them anyway because that was as close as she would ever get.

CHAPTER 20

"Head baker of tart week is… Brennen Petersen. Congratulations on being the second of this group to make head baker twice in the competition." The judge smiled, and Brennen nodded, unable to wipe the grin from his face. He shared a look with Lexi, and a little zing shot through him. She had a smile that could make even a dark night bright.

Where had that thought come from?

Once they were done, he moved to clean up his workspace, grateful Lexi had done quite a bit already. As he took the washcloth and wiped the mixer down, he watched as she cleaned out the bowls and tools, using her fingernail to scratch at a spot here and there. She was so meticulous and clean about everything. But then again, that's what made her a great baker. He'd never tried any of her food, but they'd just started sharing more personal details about one another.

Where does she work? They'd been working together for the past five weeks, and he didn't even know that yet. He'd been meaning to ask her, wanting to try something she made rather than food she'd directed him to make.

"Congrats, Brennen. Did you listen to everything I said?" she smirked, her eyes twinkling as she looked up at him.

"I might have forgotten a few things, but at least I made head baker." He paused, searching her eyes for something even he wasn't sure of. Maybe some acknowledgement she felt the same way he did. "What are you doing tonight? Do you want to celebrate?"

Her face took on a somber look, and her eyes looked like saucers. "Um, well, there's a family event I need to get to." She untied her apron and folded it up, stuffing it under the island. "But, um, you can come if you want."

Brennen studied her features, trying to see if she was joking or not. They'd been teasing each other a lot in the past few days, and he liked the lighthearted banter and the easy conversation.

"What's it for?"

"My sister's engagement party. My mom is going all out, like she always does with family functions, so it might be too much for you."

He held a hand up and said, "Oh, no. You're fine. I just didn't want it to be super formal and have me intrude. Is everyone dressing up?"

She gave him a look of surprise. "A button-up shirt and some slacks would work, I think." He saw her throat move in a big gulp as she continued to stare at him.

"What time? Send me the address, and I'll come. Do you want me to pick you up?"

"I, uh, I, well, no. I'll just meet you there." A flush covered her cheeks, and she looked away, embarrassed. Pulling out her phone, she started typing and a few seconds later, his phone dinged. She waved to him as she scrambled out the door.

Brennen wasn't sure what to make of it. He'd never seen her so flustered.

He was even surprised he'd said yes. They hadn't even been on a real date and here he was meeting her family. That was his fault, and he'd have to remedy that. Because he was ready to take a step forward. Was she though?

CHAPTER 21

"What was I thinking asking him?" Lexi said aloud to herself as she walked to the T-station. She checked her watch and calculated four hours until the beginning of the party. By the time she got home, she'd have threeish left and, knowing her mother, she'd be called down to help with food preparations. Not to mention, she needed to finish the pastries she'd started that morning. Brennen wouldn't come near her with a ten-foot pole after this.

She was still shocked he'd agreed to come along to a family party. Stopping abruptly, a flood of dread fell over her. Who was she kidding? He wouldn't come near her again after meeting her family. Was she testing him subconsciously?

Her family's behavior wasn't something she could put stock in, and Garrett had only been around her immediate family twice at most. The one benefit to having him there was that he would pull her mom off her scent at least a little. She didn't need poor Aaron to be dragged into the restaurant again.

Stepping off the T, she hurried to her home, barging through the door at a quick walk. It would be easier to get the desserts done and then shower so she wouldn't have to worry about smelling like fried food.

Coming around the corner and into the kitchen, she heard her mother ordering people about, her words meshing together at the speed she delivered them. "No, Johnny, that doesn't go over there. We need to put them in this basket so it can go right onto the table. Sergio, are you almost done with the meat?"

Lexi was glad she'd taken the time to prepare most of the ingredients before the bake-off. She'd whipped the cream that morning for the tres leches cake, but she still needed to frost it. The frosting for the six dozen cupcakes sat in a large bowl, waiting for her to decorate. She'd also made picarones and was excited at the thought of Brennen trying out her baking. Or any of her family, for that matter. At least her mom hadn't contracted the shops down the road.

She buzzed through, glancing up to see she'd done it all within two hours. It took another fifteen minutes to get them all on platters out on the long table, but she took a step back, admiring her work.

Her mother came out and looked along the table. "These look really good, hija. Bien hecho." Lexi grinned, satisfaction flowing through her body. It was the first real compliment her mother had ever given her about her desserts. There had been a few times when she'd run the restaurant while her father was recovering that her mother said she was grateful, which was a huge step coming from Angelica Sarmiento.

"Alexis, please tell me that's not what you're wearing to the party?"

That didn't last long.

"I'm not wearing this. I was planning on taking a shower.

What time is it?" Lexi had left her phone in the kitchen, and the large room didn't have a clock.

"You have forty-five minutes. We are starting this party on time, so you'd better get going."

Lexi ran upstairs and down the hall. The bathroom door was closed, and she could hear water. Pounding on it, she said, "You have five minutes. I need to get in there."

The water stopped, and a few seconds later, the door opened. Sophie looked out, her hair twisted in a towel on top of her head. "Excuse you. You can't just rush home and demand things like that. Go use the other one."

"You're done for now. I'll hurry and shower and then do my hair in my room." Lexi took off down the hallway, running to grab underwear and figure out what she would wear. She'd worn her red polka dot dress the night of speed dating, so she couldn't wear that again. She moved one hanger at a time, hoping that something in her wardrobe would be perfect for the occasion.

The extended Sarmiento family was coming. She couldn't try too hard, or they would know something was up. She wanted to throw people off her single status, not drag Brennen through the mud of interrogation that was sure to come.

Opting for a plum-colored blouse with puffed sleeves and a gray pencil skirt, she ran back down the hall, tapping her foot until Sophie left, her sister sticking her tongue out as she walked past.

With a quick shower and smooth legs a few minutes later, she was back in her room. As she worked to straighten out the kinks of her hair, she couldn't leave it straight. Taking pieces, she made several pin curls along the sides of her face and then twirled the bottom, pinning it up in back. It was elegant and still had enough of her style to make her not want to hide completely. Throwing on a pair of flats, she trudged down to the restaurant, hearing a buzz of activity already.

She snuck into the room, hoping to avoid the gaze of her family. She wasn't up to hearing her mother's take on Lexi's choice in style. Casting her eyes around the room, she looked for a familiar set of hazel eyes. Instead, she found her mother staring at her feet.

"Where are your heels? Go get them now."

"Ma, I can move so much easier in these."

She shook her head. "Maybe, but you need to catch a man. Here, take mine." Stepping out of her heels, her mother waited for Lexi to move. "I'll wear yours until I can run upstairs and change."

"Ma, I'm a grown woman. I can make these decisions for myself. And right now, my feet need comfort."

Her mother waved her hand and shook her head. "You won't find a man unless you're wearing heels."

Ready to be done with this argument and knowing her mother was nowhere near budging, Lexi stepped into the heels, feeling like she'd just gone up an elevator. Looking down at her flats on her mother, with the sparkly sequined dress, it looked odd.

"Really, Ma, let me go up and change. I invited some—"

"Go mingle, Alexis. There are plenty of people here who aren't related to you." She winked, and Lexi threw up in her mouth. That's all she could picture when she turned around, talking to someone until she found out they were related. She'd only gone about three steps when her balance shifted wrong in the shoes, and she bumped into someone.

Looking up, she saw the blue flecked with green eyes and looked down to see her hands pressed up against his hard chest. She dropped her hands and took a step back, wobbling a bit to avoid hitting someone else. Brennen reached out and grabbed her arm, keeping her from falling over backwards.

"Thank you," she said, regaining her balance on the heels.

"Those add some height. I'm not used to seeing you almost shoulder high." He laughed, and her stomach flipped at the sound.

She looked down at the shoes, wishing for her flats. "These are my mother's. She was mad I wasn't wearing any, so she made me wear these. She claims that a way to hook a guy is through his stomach and these stilts."

"Stilts. That's funny." His laughter caused her to crack a smile. He looked around and pointed to the crowd. "This is crazy. Are all these people your family?"

Lexi took in the room with fresh eyes, realizing that a guy with only a sister would think this was all chaos. "Not all, but most. It gets crazy here with all of us, but what good is a restaurant if you can't entertain people?"

He nodded, his smile wide enough to show his teeth. "So, this is where you learned how to cook, huh? But baking, no?" He brought his hand up to his face, resting his chin between his thumb and forefinger.

"A little here and there, but my mom does most of the desserts on the menu, all Peruvian. I had to get out to learn all about the different kinds and the specialties worldwide."

They stood in silence, staring out at the crowd. Brennen turned and looked at her hands, then back to her face. "Are you thirsty? Can I grab you something?"

"Just a water, thank you."

"Okay, I'll be right back." She watched him navigate through the crowd, and her heart thumped several beats faster. She could get used to someone like him around.

Loud sounds came from down the hall, and Lexi knew her thoughts had come too soon. Through the door came Kathy and Jacqueline, dressed more scandalously than a pop princess and a groupie. Lexi rolled her eyes, not in the mood for their antics. Of course, their mother lavished them with kisses and praise right then, telling them they looked amazing.

Lexi wobbled over to a seat and pulled off a heel. It was at least an inch bigger than the tallest ones she wore. How could her mother stand such things?

"Here you go." Brennen held out a bottled water, and Lexi took it gratefully. "So, does your family party like this all the time?" He took a sip of soda, and Lexi was transfixed by the movement of his lips until she remembered he'd asked her a question.

"Often enough. It gets annoying after a while. So, I usually make an appearance and then hide out in my room."

His expression turned thoughtful. "Do you live close to here?"

He'll find out soon enough. She pointed to the ceiling.

"Wow, that's close. At least if you're hungry in the middle of the night, you have a full-size grill."

"Yeah, but what I want is someone else to make it for me." She chuckled, knowing how true it was. After taking over for those six months, she was surprised her parents had made it decades running the restaurant.

"Do you have a favorite chef or pastry chef? How does that work? Is it like athletics where you have a favorite player?"

Lexi chuckled. "No. But my favorite is Pierre Roux. I've never tried his cooking, but I hear he has some amazing dishes. I've watched every episode of his cooking show and am always mesmerized."

"Do you mean the Pierre who cooks at Top Shelf?" When Lexi nodded, he continued, "You've never been there?"

"Are you kidding? The wait list is months long. I think I'll finally be able to eat there when I'm forty." She laughed a little and ended with a snort. Brennen laughed harder, and she couldn't help but follow.

When they'd settled down, he waved toward the table of food. "Should we get some food? There's something here that's making my mouth water just from the smell."

"Sounds good. It's best to get some before my mother starts with her speech. We might die of starvation if we wait too long."

He stood and put his hand out for hers, pulling her up. One hand moved to the small of her back, and the other rested on her elbow, helping her balance on the skyscraper shoes. She'd never felt so protected or taken care of. If this was how guys were supposed to treat gals, she'd been missing out.

"Thanks," she said, her breath catching as she glanced up at him. Lexi Sarmiento was falling for a guy, and she just hoped her heart could take whatever happened this time.

CHAPTER 22

*L*exi cringed as her mother continued to rattle off in Spanglish to a somewhat captivated audience about how amazing Richard would be as a son-in-law, and she hoped she'd be a grandmother soon. She must have had a lapse in judgment when she thought it would be okay to invite Brennen to a family party. He probably thought they were all nuts.

Once the speeches were done and everyone was mingling about the room, Lexi held her stomach and said, "I think I ate too much."

"Well, you look great." Heat rushed to his cheeks at his awkward delivery, and she smiled. Trying to change the conversation a bit, he said, "Everything was delicious. I'm glad your mother likes garlic. It's such a great flavor."

Is that a hint to stay away from kissing him? Or does he think I'm suddenly a vampire?

Her worst nightmare was coming to pass as she watched her youngest sisters make their way towards them, a predatory look on their faces.

"Lexi, who is your hot friend?" Leave it to them to boil all her feelings down to something so immature. There were so many other words in the English, and Spanish language for that matter, to describe someone's attractiveness.

Holding her hand out, she said, "This is Brennen Petersen. I'm his baking teacher."

Jacqueline raised one eyebrow and tried to be seductive. "I had no idea what kind of perks there were to being a baker. You've been holding out on us, Lexi."

Brennen reached out his hand and grasped Lexi's, squeezing it a moment. The action was startling, but the sensation covered her like a warm bubble bath, and she loved it.

Her youngest sister cringed as her eyes fell to where their hands were connected. "Well, it seems the Dateless Woman has taken off her cape. Come on, Jackie. I think I saw some cute guys over in the other corner." The two of them left, emphasizing their walk as if trying to get the attention of everyone in the room.

Lexi looked down at their hands, and Brennen followed her gaze. He left his warm palm surrounding hers for a moment or two and then pulled back. It wasn't a real slap in the face, but all she wanted was a few moments alone in her bedroom, where she could curl up and get past the memories of her time with Garrett, all the insecurities that had built up over the past year. For a moment, she'd believed she had made it past all the anxiety of relationships, the constantly questioning every move.

"Thanks, for that." She gave him half a smile, and he smiled back.

"No problem. Dateless Woman, huh? That sounds like a tough nickname."

Lexi shrugged, studying her hands. "I told you the gist of my dating life. The nickname is almost a running joke around my family."

"What's that?" Brennen turned his head, as if listening for something. With the room near packed with people, she wasn't sure what had caught his attention.

And then she heard it. High-pitched and off-key, Sophie's voice singing some old-time love ballad. Closing her eyes and dropping her head, shame washed over her.

Yep, he won't be coming around after this.

"Are you all right?"

"If you mean wishing for the floor to open and swallow me whole, then yes, I'm all right. That would be the middle sister, regaling us with her lack of talent in the musical department." She looked up and bit her lip, all the feelings for this guy roaring to life while seeing in his face the discomfort of the situation.

He laughed, but it sounded forced, not like the deep rumble he usually had when they were baking.

"I told you we're all sorts of crazy here. Some of us more than others."

Ceila and Richard walked in their direction and when her sister saw Lexi standing so close to Brennen, her eyes flew open wider, and she looked like she was ready to squeal. Pulling Lexi into a hug, she whispered, "Who's the guy? He's gorgeous."

Through gritted teeth, Lexi whispered, "I'll tell you later."

People called for the engaged couple from the other side of the room, so Ceila pulled back and looked at Brennen. "Our family isn't the best at first impressions but give her a chance, and you won't regret it."

Lexi's stomach dropped. She must have been wishing for the death of any future relationship with Brennen when she'd invited him. Why was her family so embarrassing?

"Do you want dessert?" Lexi asked. She would need every bit of sugar on the table to survive this party. She got a plate for them, grabbing a couple of the desserts she'd made.

"Did you make these?" he said after one bite of the Peruvian dessert.

Lexi frowned, unable to see if this would be positive or negative. "Why?"

"Because these are incredible. I've never had anything like it."

"I made them. Picarones are my favorite. They're popular in Peru, and I learned to make them from my grandmother when I was small. It's an old family tradition."

He smiled as he took another bite. After he swallowed, he said, "This is the best pastry I've ever had." He seemed to see her in a new light from his expression. But was that just validation for her knowing her stuff when it came to baking? Or was he feeling that same magnetism between them that made it hard for her to fight the distance when she was near him?

"I'm glad you think so."

Brennen glanced at his watch, a frown tugging on the corners of his mouth. "I'm sorry, but I have to run. My sister is leaving for a summer camp in the morning, and I want to say goodbye before she leaves. But I'll see you at our next practice, right?"

Walking him to the door of the restaurant, she nodded, longing to hug him, to feel his strong arms around her. But instead, she opened the door, smiling at him.

"Thanks for coming tonight. I know my family is odd, but thanks for helping me stave off the humiliation of being set up again."

He laughed, the deep rumble making her knees go weak. "I'm glad. I know how it is for people to try to set me up. Then again, I don't usually go on the dates, so there's that."

"Maybe I'll send my mother over for a few days, and you can see what I go through."

Raising his hands, he said with a grin, "No, no. I have Clara, and she's as much as I can handle right now. Just let me know if I can rescue you again." He tipped his head forward, giving her a look to say he was serious.

"Deal."

"Cakes, right?" It took her a minute to register what he meant by that, until she remembered it was the theme for next week's bake-off.

"Yep." They smiled for one awkward moment before he leaned in, wrapping his arms around her. Electricity sparked in just about every nerve ending in her body, and the smell of his cologne only heightened the moment. And then he stepped back, waving as he walked out the door and down the street.

She was falling for him. She'd tried not to, but the pull of his magnetic smile and nearly teal eyes drew her in. If she could hide it for a few more weeks until the competition ended, she'd probably never see him again. But he'd hugged her, and for longer than was normal for just a friendly gesture. She was going to get hurt, but she couldn't stop the downward slide of emotions. Next stop: Heartbreak Canyon.

CHAPTER 23

*H*e should have kissed her.

Brennen had thought about the hug over the next few days, every time kicking himself for not leaning down to kiss Lexi's bright red lips. But when he'd seen her mother come around the corner, he'd panicked, not wanting an audience for his first kiss in way too long.

Her family had its quirks, but after being without his parents for so many years, he missed the fun more people could bring. And now that Clara wouldn't be spending the summer with him, he craved that interaction even more.

She'd had to cancel their practice session on Monday, and so he was behind on learning about cakes. At least they were easier than biscuits.

Wednesday came around, and the goal was a three-tiered chocolate cake and so far, they hadn't made great progress.

"I had no idea baking entailed this much thought and work," he said, scooping batter into the prepared pan. "I guess I thought that anyone could bake. Then again, I burned Clara's cake for her sixteenth birthday, and I'd used a boxed cake mix. I haven't attempted a cake since."

Lexi laughed, sending tingles through him. "How did you burn it?"

"I put it in a small pan, so the batter overflowed. I think remnants of it are still at the bottom of the oven."

"You haven't cleaned it? In three years?" Her eyes were wide with shock, and Brennen gave her a sheepish grin.

"Well, it's not like I use the oven a whole lot, if ever. I'm lucky I use the stovetop occasionally."

Her lips twisted to the side, and her eyebrows cinched together as she stared at him. "Don't you get sick of eating out?"

He hadn't thought about it until then, as eating out was the only way to eat except for ramen noodles and mac and cheese. "Yeah, but how else am I supposed to eat?"

"It's called learning how to cook. Just like you've been doing here with baking."

"Yeah, I guess you're right. I can see how cooking would be a good skill to master." He finished pouring the flour into a large bowl and as he was about to put the lid on, he took a pinch of the white stuff between his fingers and tossed it at Lexi, coating her nose and eyelashes.

Her reaction at first made him laugh, fury crossing her face as she wiped at her eyes. With one swift motion, she scooped up a handful of flour from the bowl and tossed it into his face, blinding him temporarily. He caught some in his mouth when it was open and coughed.

"I'm sorry! Are you all right?" Lexi's hand rested on his shoulder as he doubled over, hiding the measuring cup half-full of flour.

He looked into her face, feigning injury. She was so close he could have kissed her lips and for a second, he debated it, before he raised the cup and tossed the contents over her head, the flour settling into her hair and coating her chin and neck. She straightened, and puffs of flour filled the air around her.

"You're dead." She tried to keep her expression fierce, but the corners of her mouth turned up. As he studied her beautiful features covered in white dust, the urge to kiss her hit him again, and he stepped forward, feeling the tension and electricity course between them.

He bent his head a little, only inches from her face when he saw her hand move out of the corner of his eye. Seconds later, he was covered in the rest of the flour he'd measured into the bowl. Standing straight, the flour fell into his eyes, some of it trailing down his back inside his shirt.

He rubbed at his eyes, the flour drying out all moisture. After blinking several times, his vision cleared, and he saw Lexi's face, a mixture of worry and happiness. She set the large bowl down and bit her bottom lip, drawing his attention for the third time in minutes.

Letting out a deep laugh, he leaned over and shook his head from side to side, sending the dust everywhere. Lexi moved back, and he pursued to the point that they were running around the room. Her laugh was more of a giggle now, and he finally caught up to her, grabbing her around the waist to pull her to a stop. She twisted in his arms until she faced him, this time the tension to unknown bounds. Her smile fell from her face as she stared at his lips.

Right as he leaned in again, someone cleared their throat. Irritated, he turned to find Charlotte with an amused expression on her face, standing by the door.

"Am I interrupting something?" she asked, trying to keep a wide grin from her face.

Lexi broke free of his arms and brushed at her sleeves and apron, sending billowing clouds to the floor. "No, we just had an accident with the flour."

"Riiight. Lex, can I steal you for a second?"

Lexi turned to him and smiled before moving in Charlotte's direction. Her usual black hair was covered in flour, making her look slightly older. As he watched her walk away, he realized he'd just missed out on the chance to kiss her. Again. Charlotte had the worst timing in the world.

* * *

"WHAT'S UP?" Lexi asked Charlotte as they stepped into the hall.

"One of the contestants is opting out of the competition. We'll be cutting one of the weeks, and I wanted to ask you which you'd prefer, pies or pastries?"

Lexi raised her eyebrows. "Is that even a question? Pastries."

"You think Lover Boy in there can survive pastry week?"

"Lover Boy? We aren't together. We haven't even been on a date." Lexi folded her arms across her chest, daring Charlotte to contradict her. The image of his soft eyes as he leaned in to kiss her was front and center in her mind. She'd been so close to seeing how his lips felt on hers.

With a sly grin, Charlotte said, "I do remember you telling me about him coming to Ceila's engagement party last weekend, right? That was a date."

"No, it wasn't."

"You invited him to come to a *family* gathering," Charlotte's emphasis on family made Lexi's stomach flip, "and he actually came? I'd say that's a date, for sure. And speed dating. That's two, girl."

Waving her hand in the air, Lexi said, "It doesn't matter. The true test of a baker is the pastry. If you want to get more donations, make the last week all about pastries."

Charlotte nodded, as if considering this. "Okay, we'll get some promos sent out and make sure we get the camera crew in for then. You better get in there and teach him how to bake a cake. He's got to make it through this week to even think about pastries."

Lexi cringed as Charlotte winked on her way out. Part of her liked the idea of dating Brennen. Okay, *all* of her *loved* the idea of dating him.

He'd been so solemn the first few times they'd met, but he was a lot more sensitive and caring than she'd originally thought. Then again, he was one of those fitness gurus, which meant he probably had interest in girls who liked that sort of thing. When was the last time she'd gone for a run?

But that hadn't stopped him from flirting with her, even if she was still covered in flour. She had a lot to offer and if he were interested in dating her, she'd accept. If not, she wasn't about to change herself completely to mold to someone else's expectation.

She walked into the room to find Brennen sweeping up the flour on the floor. Placing her hand over her heart, she felt the strength of each beat as it pounded against her chest. She might have underestimated her feelings for him. But did he even remotely feel the same?

CHAPTER 24

*B*rennen kept finding excuses to text or talk to Lexi over the next few days. Now that they'd opened up a bit to each other, she was easy to talk to, and he needed someone like that in his life, even if she only wanted to be friends.

He'd survived cake week, but only barely. He'd gotten distracted and forgot how many tablespoons of cocoa he'd put into the cake. From the taste, he'd almost doubled it. The small forkful he'd tried was so bitter, the chocolate frosting couldn't even save it.

The redeeming part was that he'd at least pulled together a baked cake. The other guy's cake had been oozing in the middle, and it wasn't supposed to be a lava cake. He wasn't happy to see that Jessica Pace was head baker, but they'd be going head to head for the final week. The other woman in the final four was nearing the end of her pregnancy and had gotten sick enough to be on bedrest at the hospital, pulling out of the bake-off.

Jessica looked at him and snickered, taking a bite of her

own cake and making the face that she was savoring it. He turned away, his competitiveness sparking a brush fire through him.

"What's wrong?" Lexi asked, raising an eyebrow.

Calm flooded his chest and he gave her a small smile. "I get a little competitive. We'll have to work hard this week, so we can win this thing. I didn't think I'd make it this far but now, it's go big or be the loser."

"Eh, I'm glad I didn't have to be her coach. Jordan said she's like this all the time."

"So, what you're saying is you're glad you got stuck with me?" Brennen batted his eyes several times, forcing a laugh from her.

"Don't push it, Cocoa Man."

Lexi shook her head, her long hair pulled halfway back and reaching down to her elbows. He liked this look on her, a t-shirt and jeans, light makeup. Such a contrast to how she was when she dressed up, although that was beautiful too. For some reason, this simple version of her reminded him of his mother, and a tingle shot up his back and down his arms.

"Honestly, I didn't think we'd still be here either. When you asked if we could just buy the canned biscuits from the store, I knew I had my work cut out for me." She gave him a serious look before a smile took over.

He laughed. "I almost asked you if we could just use a cake mix." The flash in her eyes before her lips curled in a grin only made him laugh harder. "I've learned a lot since then, that's for sure."

"Then I'm doing my job."

Charlotte walked over, handing Lexi a paper with a sly smile. Lexi ignored her and read whatever was on the paper. Brennen moved so he was reading over her shoulder, liking that she'd leaned back into him an inch or two.

"Look! You're killing Jessica in contributions. Hopefully, we can get the pastries figured out and have you win. She's been so smug this whole time, and I have to work not to throw a rolling pin at her."

At least I'm not the only one.

She turned to look at him and as he thought of an attempt to kiss her again, her voice echoed in his mind, from the day she said she couldn't abide liars.

"Lexi, there's something I need to tell you."

The look on her face went from worry, to suspicion in only a few seconds. "What is it?"

"I'm not—"

"Brennen Petersen? Yeah, I already know."

He shook his head. He'd almost forgotten about his second pen name. "Wait, what? How do you know about that? Are you mad at me for lying about it?"

She shook her head slowly, as if still wrestling with the idea. "No, I get why you did it. You're the wealthy half-recluse, son of philanthropist parents who started this charity. Is that why you joined the bake-off?"

"It was more of an assignment from my editor at first. But when I got here that first day, it was an opportunity to give back on something that was dear to my mother's heart."

"From these numbers," she held up the paper for him to see, "it seems like you're doing a great job of it."

He turned his head an inch, trying to judge her overall feeling. "So, you're not mad then?"

She laughed, that tinkling sound hitting home. Now he just needed to come clean about the other alter ego, the one she'd seemed so curious about all those weeks ago. He just hoped she'd be as chill about that one as she was about the extra letters he'd added to his last name.

"I'm also—"

Her phone rang, and she held up a finger, mouthing, "Sorry" to him. It was just as well. The one admission of the day had already done a number on him. He'd tell her tomorrow about Noah Parsons and hope she forgave him.

CHAPTER 25

The phone rang the next afternoon and when Brennen saw Lexi's name, he smiled. Picking up, he said, "Hey. How's it going? I was just on my way over for our practice."

Her voice came through a bit strangled. "Change of plans. The girl who covers the night shift called in sick. Can you meet me at my work?"

"Yeah, sure. Just send me the address." He clicked off and waited for the text to come through. It was a lot closer to where he'd had lunch than he'd thought, and he got out of his car, deciding to walk rather than hunt for a parking spot.

He walked out from the shadow of a building and saw several food trucks in the area but no other brick and mortar restaurants. Did she work in a food truck? The idea didn't compute in his brain, and he checked the address again. She had all this experience baking, but she worked at a food truck?

He read every number in the address one at a time, glancing up at the numbers on surrounding buildings. It was the right place.

143

Since there were several trucks, he walked up to each, peering in to see if Lexi was working. He felt like a creeper, but what could he do?

Then he saw the old-style van, the one with the light-pink paint job and baked goods drawn all over it. Now that he saw it, everything clicked. Her old-school style and pastries. How had he not figured this out before?

He sat on a bench nearby, running both hands through his hair. His heart pounded, and he understood now all her questions about Noah Parsons. Only an owner would be so defensive. That was why he hadn't wanted to write about food trucks in the first place. It was so personal to them. But now it was personal to him too. He was one step away from loving that girl, the one smiling at a customer as she handed them some twisted pastry. And she was about to hate him for his anonymous words.

After a moment of indecision, where he thought he'd run away, he walked up to the window of the van. But he'd tried her pastries, and they were amazing. What had happened the day he'd originally visited the truck?

"Hey." He saw her at the other end, next to the small counter near the front, busy getting something ready. She turned and smiled at him.

"Go around and come in the door." She pointed to the backside of the van and turned back to the counter.

Once inside, the smells of yeast, fresh baked bread, and pastries threw him. "You never told me you owned a food truck."

She turned with a smile and put her arms outstretched to encompass it all. "I didn't tell you a lot of things. Mostly because you were a jerk the first time I met you."

"And now?" Brennen quirked an eyebrow and waited, holding his breath.

"I think you're a pineapple."

"Huh?" This conversation wasn't going the way he wanted it to. But how did he want it to go? Mostly, he wanted to explain his pen name, the article, and anything else he'd forgotten to tell her, in the hopes that she would forgive him, and they could keep moving forward.

Lexi laughed. "Like a pineapple. You try to have this tough outer shell to ward people off but inside, you're this sweet, caring guy."

Running his hand through his hair and then rubbing the back of his neck, he debated whether he should tell her. As much as he hated to reveal his pen name, this was the girl he was falling for, the one who he could see a future with. She had to know he was the one behind the article. Would she forgive him though? She'd easily forgiven him about his last name change, but when she knew the truth, could she so easily get over it? He hadn't been kind in the article, but that was the biggest question of all.

"Lexi, you should know that—"

She put a finger up and walked over to the window, taking someone's order. His mind ran through the scenarios of how to tell her and how she'd react, some of them show-casing her crying abilities. Others of her shouting at him and throwing him out of her food truck.

Once the line had gone again, she walked over to the counter, pulling out a bowl filled with dough from what looked like a proofer.

"Pastries. That is the final challenge. If you can master these, you deserve to be the head baker for the competition."

He opened his mouth to explain, but she turned back to the dough, rolling it out and cutting pieces of butter, letting it drop on top of the dough. She folded it in half and used the rolling pin again. Cutting up more butter, he now understood why desserts were so good.

"How long have you had this truck?" He leaned up against

the counter, watching her work as she moved the dough with sure hands.

"Close to a year, I think. It took time to fix it up, paint the outside, and make it useable for a food truck. I worked on it after working at the restaurant all day." Her ponytail swayed as she worked, the curls still there even with the humidity and heatwave they'd been having in the city.

Brennen nodded, tucking that into his head. "What made you decide on a food truck? Why not a full-out bakery? And how did you go from law school to this?" He tried to keep his tone neutral.

"I was nearing the end of my first year of law school when I realized I didn't want to be a lawyer. I was always baking things for study groups, and I found that was what I loved. It was something different but creative, and I needed that over memorizing old law cases for future use.

"I called up my parents and told them I was enrolling in the CIA, which is a huge joke because in my case, it means Culinary Institute of America." They both chuckled before she continued, "I met Charlotte there, and we graduated two years later. I worked at La Crème for a little over a year before deciding I wanted to buy a food truck."

"You worked at Le Crème and quit? I guess I shouldn't be surprised you worked there because of your talent." Brennen stared at her like she was some fossil he'd never seen before. "Parker said Meg had been on the waiting list for several months just for the event room."

"I forget you're such good friends with Parker. Yeah, I was the assistant pastry chef. At first, it seemed like my dream job, one I could move up in. While it was great pay, I still felt constricted, like I had at law school. I realized what I wanted was the thrill of owning my own business. Creating and planning my own desserts helped with that fact too."

She shook her head and rolled her eyes. "My parents

weren't happy about it. They come from the old-school restaurant owners who think food trucks are gross and dirty. But that won't happen in my truck!" She tilted her head back and stuck out her chin, tempting Brennen to kiss her.

"I have to say, I was in that boat too, but from the looks of this place, everything is neat and accounted for."

"We get inspected every so often, but I don't want to serve anything but the best. And I can't work in a dirty environment anyway."

"Do you do all of the baking here?"

She shook her head. "No, I use the back end of the kitchen at my parents' restaurant for the bigger stuff. It's hard to have a full-sized mixer in here so I get up early in the morning to get the doughs made and then get as much done as I can before opening the truck at eight. I'm sure I could make more money by opening earlier and serving coffee, but there's only so much a girl can do, ya know?"

When she pointed at the dough, he took her place, nervous to ruin it. In Lexi's eyes, the pastry was the most important part of baking. She'd mentioned it once, saying it was time consuming, and cutting corners would result in subpar pastry. As she instructed him over the next hour, he was surprised to find that with a little elbow grease and some time, he could possibly pull it off.

What he'd failed to do was reveal his true identity. Would she forgive him once she found out?

CHAPTER 26

Why was Brennen being so weird?

They were back at the baking school, working on the equivalent of the Napoleon. Brennen seemed flustered and distant, lacking the usual joking flair Lexi had become accustomed to. She was teaching him how to make phyllo dough, and he wasn't doing anything right on it.

"Have you ever had anyone say something bad about you before meeting you?" he asked in a strained voice.

"I guess so. Why?" The question caught her off guard, and she wondered where this was coming from.

He tried to start over with the dough, making a bigger mess than when he started. "What did you do? Did you get mad about it?"

She sat back in thought, and he fidgeted with the steel mixing bowl, waiting for her answer. "I can't really remember now, but I know that it depends on what they're talking about. If it's my style, I just let it roll off. There are a lot of people who think I'm weird for what I wear and how I look, but I like it. It's different and fun. If it's about my baking, that's another story." She reflected on the article, irritation webbing through her chest.

"Have you ever forgiven the people who insulted your baking?" His voice sounded off, like he was trying to reveal something slowly.

"Why are we talking about this?"

"Well, I wanted to—"

The door clanged open and in walked Kathy and Jacqueline. Lexi groaned inwardly and cringed when they barely acknowledged Brennen. "Lexi, what are you doing?" Kathy asked in a snide tone.

"Baking, duh. Why are you two here? You're never around when I bake. Or when I have to do any manual labor, for that matter." Lexi leaned back against the counter and narrowed her eyes in their direction for emphasis.

Jacqueline clapped her hands together, practically bouncing on her toes. "We were in the neighborhood and wanted to drop by to show you something."

What in the world would they want to show her? They never spoke more than a few sentences to each other at home, and now they were dropping by the cooking school to chat? Something was off.

Drying her hands on a towel, Lexi walked over to them after giving Brennen a few words of encouragement. Resting her hand on her hip, she gave them a wave. "What is it?"

Kathy held out her left hand, and a diamond ring sat on an important finger. Lexi grabbed her sister's hand and pulled it forward, inspecting the diamond.

"Is this what I think it is?"

"I'm engaged, Lexi. Isn't it the best?" Kathy's smile turned Lexi's stomach.

"Who proposed?"

"Aaron. We're in love, and we're getting married in two months. Before Ceila's wedding for sure."

Lexi shook her head as if that would help her wake up from the horrendous nightmare. "Because getting married before your oldest sister is the most important thing about the wedding?"

"Of course not, Lexi." Kathy frowned, etching a deep line in her forehead. "He's a soldier and will be going overseas for six months. We wanted to get married before he leaves."

"You've known this guy for how long?"

Jacqueline spoke up, eager to be part of the conversation. "They've been dating about two weeks now."

Throwing her hands in the air, Lexi shook her head. "Are you serious? You can't possibly know all you need to about him in that short of time."

"What would you know? It's been years since you've dated a guy longer than a week. I came here to ask if you'd make my wedding cake but if you're going to be snippy, maybe I won't."

The words stabbed like a knife into Lexi's chest. It hadn't been years, but it almost felt like that since Garrett left. But this was her sister. She'd do what she could to support her, even if she didn't believe the marriage would last much longer than the wedding. "I'll do it. Just promise me you'll give me at least seventy-two hours' notice if the wedding is called off."

"As if that would happen," Kathy scoffed. "Okay, plan on August eighteenth." The two girls sashayed out the door without a goodbye.

"Will do." Lexi's tone sounded more reluctant to her own ears. Turning, she shifted back to the island, remembering Brennen had been there for the whole encounter. He seemed to be around for all the awkward moments in her life these days.

"Is everything okay?" he asked, pulling his hands from the dough, bits of it stuck to his fingers.

"No, it's not. But I can't fix it." What she wanted was for him to pull her close so she could get a better sense of his beachy cologne, protecting her from the hailstorm of life that was about to hit the Sarmiento home. But he didn't move close, didn't make any movements to comfort her, and she felt the void.

Her mind reflected over the questions he'd asked before her sisters had arrived. What had he done that would upset her? Because that was the only reason he'd be asking.

CHAPTER 27

*B*rennen had heard the entire conversation, the worry in Lexi's voice, and he wanted to do something to help. But her answers to his supposedly vague questions made it clear she wouldn't forgive him.

He was grateful to be home and that his sister was mostly normal. Since she'd gone, he'd felt the loneliness creep in, but she was nothing compared to Lexi's sisters.

She had a feisty streak that could extend at least to Texas, and his dumb decision to bash a food truck because it wasn't an actual restaurant in his mind at the time came back to bite him.

His phone rang, and he was surprised to see it was Clara calling for a video chat. "Hey, sis. What are you doing? I thought you wouldn't have service for the summer."

"We're out in the town for a night out, and I had a few bars, so I thought I'd check in. How are things?"

"Good, going good."

"Liar. I can see it all over your face. You're worried about something." This was why he hated video chats, he couldn't hide anything. Then again, it was nice to have someone who could see the situation from the outside and give him feedback.

It only took a few minutes to update her on the review article and how he found out Lexi owned the truck. He told her about the questions he'd tried to ask Lexi, and Clara laughed.

"Pull off the band-aid, Bren. That's the only way to know how she'll react. Then you can go from there. You'll know how to pick up the pieces and say you're sorry when it blows over."

"How do you know I want it to work? I don't, I'm curious about your assumptions." He tried to make his voice light, but he hoped he wasn't quite so transparent already. If he fell all the way for Lexi, and he was so close to doing so, he didn't need to have everyone and their dog knowing about his epic failure at love when she couldn't forgive him.

"Because you wouldn't be worrying about it if you didn't want a relationship with her." Clara's triumphant grin made him shake his head.

Thinking back to how spoiled her sisters were, his mind whirred. He'd enjoyed the time he'd had at the party with her family, but overhearing the conversation they'd had in the food truck made him wary.

"I don't know if it would work out. Her family is over the top crazy, and I'm not using that lightly. Her mom stared us down as I left the engagement party the other night, and her younger sister just got engaged to a guy she's been dating for two weeks."

"Families aren't perfect, Bren. If you like her that much, you'll figure out how to make it all work."

A sage piece of advice. "How did you get so wise?"

"By making a few mistakes and listening to you." She smiled at him. Some people in the background waved her over, and she turned back. "I've got to run, Bren. The van is leaving to go back to camp, but I'll talk to you again soon, okay?"

"Sounds good. Just don't fall in love with another counselor." It was a half-truth, half-joke, and she read right through it as she cast him a disgusted glare.

"Says the guy falling for his baking coach. Don't impede love. Just go with it." She smiled and waved at him before the screen went black.

He sat on the couch and clicked on the TV. When nothing interesting was on, he turned it off and went to his room. It had been a few days since he'd gotten a workout in. He usually had his best breakthroughs and ideas come when he was working out. Maybe the magical fix-all would reveal itself while he burned some calories.

CHAPTER 28

"I think I'm in the friend zone. Like officially." Lexi could hear the whining in her own voice and wanted to cry because of it. Since when had she become such a sap?

Charlotte pushed back a piece of the ponytail covering Lexi's face and rubbed her back. "You're not in the friend zone. What makes you think that?"

"He hasn't tried to ask me out again or even flirt. It's like I'm back to being just the coach, and I hate it. Why didn't you tell me this was how I would feel after two dates?"

"At least you're admitting it now. There's only so much I can say about dating until you've experienced it. Do you really think he doesn't like you like that?" Charlotte gave her a half-smile, and Lexi let out a sob.

She threw out her arms a bit more dramatically than intended and said, "We've almost kissed at least twice now, and the electricity between us could land one of us in the hospital for lightning shock, but now it's like I'm a stranger to him. What spooked him all of a sudden?"

"Men. We'll never know, I'm afraid. But you can ask him." Charlotte looked so confident in that.

Lexi looked at her friend in disbelief. "Me? Ask him what happened? Yeah, that'll go over well." As she said it, she remembered he'd tried to tell her something, but they kept getting interrupted.

"It's better than pretending we're still in junior high, and we can't actually tell the person we like that we like them, because what if they don't like us and turn the whole school against us?"

Lexi held out her hands, surprised by the frustration coming from her best friend. "Okay, wow. That sounded like you'd thought it out before saying it."

"I did, actually. Because it's true. We're almost thirty, Lex. We've got to be bold and ask where we stand so we don't get stuck in limbo, or as you so lovingly call it, the friend zone. Let's make a bet."

Lexi groaned. She usually lost when Charlotte came up with things like this.

"I'll bet you dinner that you don't ask him what's going on?" Charlotte's chin lifted, a challenging smile directed at Lexi.

"Dinner is all you've got going for an incentive?"

Charlotte smirked at her. "The Lexi I know doesn't walk away from a good meal. Do you accept?"

Lexi stuck out her hand. "Yes, I do. Pull out your credit card because we're flying to New York. That's what I'm picking."

Storming out of the room, Lexi stopped by the bathroom to make sure she didn't look scary with dripping mascara and then marched into the classroom, ready to take on whatever Brennen had to say in their next lesson.

* * *

HE STOOD THERE in all his chiseled glory, and Lexi had to take a few breaths before she approached him, focusing on a free dinner as the prize.

"Do you like me?"

Brennen's eyebrows cinched together, confusion and panic taking over his features. "Huh?"

"You suffered through an engagement party with my family, and we almost kissed twice during our flour escapades. Do you like me?" She could feel the heat rising up her neck and throughout her face. She probably looked like a strawberry at this point.

"Yeah, I like you."

"Then why have you been so weird since then? It's like we went from fun and flirty to strangers overnight." Her voice had raised somewhat, the emotion got caught up in it.

"I haven't been weird."

"You've been weird. And what was with all those questions the other day?" Lexi folded her arms and dipped her head, hoping the look was demanding.

Brennen rubbed both hands over his face, causing the front section of his hair to stand up. "I have something to tell you, and I don't want you to freak out."

"Well, that's probably not the best way to start a confession then, is it?" She scrunched her nose and waited, hoping it wasn't as bad as she thought it would be.

"I'm Noah Parsons."

She felt her lungs deflate and she sunk into a chair a foot away. "Excuse me? What do you mean, you're Noah Parsons?"

"That's one of my pen names. It's easier to get a real grasp of a restaurant if people don't know who I am. I started using it a few years ago, and only a handful of people know about it."

Biting her bottom lip, she could feel the same heat from

before, only anger and frustration surged. "So, you sit behind a screen and spout all of these negative reviews about people without thinking about the people themselves? Do you know how long that article has haunted me? I'm still losing sleep over it." She stood and paced back and forth.

"Please, Lexi. Please forgive—"

"That's why you kept asking if I would forgive." The words were like the last piece of the puzzle; once clicked into place, she could see the whole picture. She stood and stepped up on her chair, so she was eye to eye with him.

"You know what? Now that I know you're him, I can tell you to your face. I don't know what your problem is with food trucks, but you need to open your eyes, Brennen. Just because your words don't affect you doesn't mean they don't hurt some poor business here in town. Some restaurants and pop-up shops are just doing their best to get a good start, and they rely on reviews to do so. There's a difference in constructive criticism and acid, and your article far outweighed the acid end."

Brennen raised his hands. "Look, I'm sorry. Yours was the first food truck I've tried. At the time, I didn't think they could be considered restaurants or eateries or what have you. But you've shown me different. That they can be clean and edible, delicious even. What can I do to make it up to you?"

A single tear rolled down her cheek, and she waved her hands in the air. "I don't know, Brennen. You're going to think I'm some crazy girl who should just let it go, but I can't. My food truck is my passion; it's something I built from the ground up and is a thriving business here in the city. It's outside the realm of the family restaurant, and it doesn't confine me to an office or to something I can't evolve with."

He reached out for her, but she backed away.

"You lied. I asked you right from the beginning if you knew Noah Parsons. But here I am, the fool, thinking I might have found someone I could spend the rest of my life with, who could support me in my dreams, and now you tell me this. Thank you for not sucking three years of my life away, but I'm done." She brushed at the tears as she walked toward the door. When he called after her, she turned and said, "I'll get Charlotte to help you with your practice time today."

CHAPTER 29

Brennen felt like a pile of crud. He'd thought confessing his true identity would make her mad but not to this extent. Normally, he figured he could just give himself a few weeks and get over her, not that he'd had to do that often. But the ache in his chest told him it wouldn't work this time. He had to find a way to make it up to her, to help her see that he was sorry.

Charlotte walked in, a sad smile on her face. "You're him, huh?"

He frowned at her, raising an eyebrow to answer the question.

"Noah Parsons. She's been ranting about you for the past seven weeks, ever since that article came out. So, what are you going to do now?"

"Do now?"

"About her?" Charlotte motioned to the door as if Lexi stood just outside, waiting to hear his answer.

"What can I do? She wouldn't listen to anything I said. Is she even going to come on Saturday?" He wouldn't be able to get through the finale if she weren't there, her steady determination willing him to do well.

Charlotte took the mess of dough and threw it in the garbage. She pulled out the flour and measured it into the mixing bowl. "You're smart. You'll figure it out."

Brennen groaned. "You know her better than anyone. What will help her forgive me, or at least listen to me?"

"The best way to forgiveness is to sacrifice something dear to keep the one you want." She smiled and turned on the mixer. "Finding a way to a big apology would be good, plus she's a huge fan of pastries. No better way to show her than through those."

His mind whirred with ideas, the slice of hope cutting through the despair he'd felt moments before. "Why did it make her so upset, the article?"

"Have you read it? I know you wrote it, but have you read it since it was published? It was harsh. Besides, baking is everything to Lexi. Her parents wanted her to do something outside of the food industry, which is why she went to law school for a bit. But her true passion is and always will be baking. She feels like her worth is contingent on her success as a baker because of it. As irrational as it sounds, when you bashed her food truck, you bashed her. It will take something creative and thoughtful to get her to break that cycle of thinking."

He watched as Charlotte worked the dough, her hands not moving as gracefully as he was used to from Lexi. Picturing her in the polka dot dress, a thought occurred to him.

"Has Lexi always dressed like that?"

"Like what? A girl from World War II? No."

"Okay, so what triggered it?" He wished she wouldn't be so tight lipped. He needed all the information he could get from her best friend.

Charlotte took in a deep breath, turning to face him directly. "Garrett almost broke her. He'd manipulated so many situations to go in his favor, it took awhile for Lexi to realize what were lies and what was truth. I think the clothes are a coping mechanism. I've seen her wear more normal clothes in the past few weeks than I have in the past four or five years."

"Why is that significant?"

"I don't know. Maybe she's ready to try love again. Didn't she say she'd thought about a future with you?"

The words ran through his mind as if on a blackboard. She had said something like that. If only he could time travel back and change the article.

The lesson passed quickly, for which he was grateful. Once he got home, he pulled out his laptop, searching for that post. As he reread the words and as he connected them to everything Charlotte had described, he knew he'd messed up, more than he originally thought.

He wanted her by his side, and the thought made his insides turn out of the gut-wrenching desire to make things right. His prejudice against food trucks, as silly as it sounded in his mind, had ruined a good chance he had at a relationship. He had to show her that he'd changed, that he saw things differently now.

Working through the night, he hoped to come up with a master plan to win her back. By the time two in the morning rolled around, he'd worked things out for the most part. All he needed was for her to show up to the finale.

CHAPTER 30

*L*exi wasn't sure where she was heading, but she knew she couldn't go straight home. She didn't need her mother's triumphant face glaring at her.

Why did she feel so awful? Because the man she loved had hurt her in a way she wasn't sure she could get over. Ever. The situation was worse than her breakup with Garrett. She tried to think of someone she could talk to, an objective person who wouldn't judge either side too quickly.

Her first choice had been Charlotte, but she'd left her in charge of Brennen's final lesson. She couldn't roam the streets of Boston for another five hours until Charlotte was done with that and with the management at the school. She didn't have many friends left from high school and didn't know how to contact most of them.

Looking at her phone, she saw it was almost three o'clock. Most of the people she knew were working. Her thoughts drifted, and two faces popped into her mind. Meg and Parker.

Sure, she didn't know Meg all that well, but she had experience working with relationships; maybe she could at least calm her down. And Parker, he knew both Lexi and Brennen. Maybe he could shed some light on who Brennen really was if everything he'd said and done had been a lie or had been for the purpose of a story.

She hopped on the T and rode out on the C-line, stopping by Harvard Ave. Walking over to the building that housed the company, Love, Austen, she was happy to see the lights were still on. Fridays were iffy for a lot of companies in the city at this hour and as she pulled open the doors, a spring scent filled her senses, helping her to relax somewhat.

A brunette behind the reception desk looked up and smiled at her. "How can I help you? Oh, hi, Lexi. How have you been?"

"Normally, things are good, Tiffany. Today, not so much. Is Meg here? I just wanted to talk to her about something."

"She is. Parker is helping her figure out something, but I'm sure they'd love to see you."

Lexi nodded her thanks and walked the few steps to Meg's office. She knocked on the door and heard Meg's voice calling to come in.

"Lexi! What a surprise. How are things?" Meg smiled but must have seen the look on Lexi's face because her expression changed to one of sympathy. "What happened, girl?" She stood behind the desk and walked over, pulling Lexi into a hug. It felt a little awkward as Meg was several inches taller. Then again, everyone was taller than she.

It reminded her of just one of the differences between her and Brennen. Tears escaped, and Parker gave her a sympathetic look from his spot behind the desk.

"What happened?" Meg pulled back, searching Lexi's face. She moved her to one of the chairs in front of the desk, and they sat down, Meg keeping her hand on Lexi's forearm.

"I think I'm in love with Brennen."

Parker chuckled but stopped short when Meg shot him a look. "I don't understand why you're so sad then. Isn't that a good thing?"

Lexi shook her head and explained about the review article and then a few of the highlights over the past few weeks. When she described what had happened only an hour before, Meg pulled her in for another hug.

"It sounds like he likes you too, Lexi. You can work it out."

"No, we can't. How am I supposed to be with someone who can be so different in person and on paper?"

Parker stood, tucking his hands into his pockets. "Honestly, Brennen is a great guy, Lexi. The two of you are a great match. He has his quirks, like everyone, but from what he's told us during our mornings on the river, he's got feelings for you too. Is there something he can do to make it up to you?"

Lexi saw the wheels spinning in his mind, and she drew in a sharp breath. "I don't know. You know all I went through when I quit law school, and a little about my relationship with Garrett. Baking is everything to me. I can't get rid of those words. It's like they're etched on my brain now."

"You're still going to the finale tomorrow though, right?" Meg gave her a look, one Lexi's mother gave way too often. It wasn't just a question, but more of a demand.

"I can't face him. Not yet."

"You love that charity, Lex. You can't let your pride get in the way of that. He'll need you there, for the support at least. He's been through a lot since his parents died. At least give him the chance to explain himself." Parker gave her a knowing look, and Lexi wondered how much of the story he already knew.

Nothing like an arrow straight to the heart. How could she show up when looking at Brennen would reduce her to tears?

Lexi dabbed a tissue under eyes and then her nose, trying

to control the wave of emotions taking over her. Part of her wanted to run to a hole and sleep for days, hoping the hurt and ache she felt would be replaced with a resolve to move forward without men in her life.

"I'll think about it."

Dread hit her stomach as she awoke the next morning. It was only nine o'clock, but she hadn't been able to fall asleep until closer to four, and her body felt like lead. Sitting up in bed, she moved her feet to the floor, her hands resting next to her as she fought a mental battle about what to do.

After a few minutes, she decided she couldn't not go to the competition. It was the last time she would have to see Brennen, and she wanted to be there when they presented a check to the owners of Project Fed.

She could be a big girl, enough to make it through a few hours of discomfort. Changing, she put on a simple day dress. She decided to leave her hair down, since she wouldn't be the one baking, and curled the ends. Applying mascara, eyeshadow, and blush, she walked out of the house, determined to be strong. She'd cried so much the day before, she'd given herself a headache and didn't need to feel that pain two days in a row.

For some reason, the outfit she now wore gave her a push of confidence, as if she were finally letting her real self shine through. She'd begun dressing like Rosie the Riveter after Garrett had dictated how she should dress for almost every event they attended together. He'd wanted a proper trophy girlfriend and when she started to put her foot down, he'd lost it.

Maybe it was the satisfaction of embarrassing him as much as he'd hurt her that had kept her in the mode of a forties woman trying to be independent in the twenty-first century. But this was promising, this freeing sense of self had been kept locked up for all this time, and it was like she was breathing new air. Something as simple as clothes.

Brennen was just another guy who thought about himself rather than the feelings of others. As she'd reread the article the night before, she'd realized why he'd been so surprised the day they'd done the lesson on the food truck. He'd remarked at the cleanliness and order, most likely believing all food trucks were the opposite.

She arrived at the school, ready for whatever came next. It was only ten minutes until filming would begin, and there was no sign of Brennen or that he'd come to prep his station. As angry as she was at him, she hoped he wasn't throwing in the towel. He'd received almost half of all the money donated to the competition, which would help sway the vote if there were some fluke chance of a tie.

Lexi turned to find Jessica staring at her, a smug look on her face. "I haven't seen him, but when you do, tell him thanks for letting me win the bake-off."

Fury ignited in her chest, and she had to force her legs to turn and walk back out before she slapped the woman across the face. She was in no mood to deal with petty people.

"Lexi, I'm so glad you made it. Come with me." Charlotte took hold of her upper arm, pulling her into the conference room near the stage.

"What's going on?" Lexi shrugged away from Charlotte's

hold and rubbed the spot where she'd been pulled. She was grateful for a lot of things her best friend did for her, but she wished everything weren't one giant surprise.

"Shh. Just watch." Lexi took a seat on one of the folding chairs, and Charlotte turned on a projector, shining on the white wall across from it. In the frame stood a large podium and several people milling behind it, but Lexi didn't recognize any of them.

Moments later, a familiar face stood behind the microphones connected to the podium, and Lexi squirmed, torn between the feelings she had for him.

"Hello, everyone. Thank you for coming today. I know time is short, and the competition for the Project Fed finale is set to air soon. I just wanted to share a few things before I go back in there and pray I can make something close to a pastry." He stopped, giving a small smile as the unseen crowd chuckled.

"After talking to my editor at Boston World, we've decided it's time to reveal that I'm the guy behind the Noah Parsons articles and reviews." The crowd made a few sounds, some of them voicing surprise that the fitness app creator would need to worry about writing articles.

"I enjoyed it while I was head of the column, but it's time for me to move to something new, a new passion I've found, thanks to an amazing woman, Alexis Sarmiento. You see, I did a review on her food truck, but my review was biased. I didn't think food trucks should be considered a restaurant, or even good food for that matter. But her passion for baking made me realize what I was lacking in life."

He looked down for a moment, as if gathering his thoughts. "For any of you who read the review on Roll With It, I urge you to stop by there yourself. Lexi is one of the most amazing bakers and pastry chefs in this town. It's got some of the best desserts in Boston, and I hope you'll give it a chance despite my article several weeks ago."

The noise level of the crowd increased for several seconds before tapering off, allowing Brennen to speak again.

"We only have a few hours left to donate to Project Fed, so please do so now. My mother was Caroline Peters, the founder of Project Fed. She started it out of a storage shed, collecting food from businesses and restaurants to help the kids of this town. And I hope to show my support for this great cause and will continue to do so long after this competition is over. The kids of Boston will benefit from this service, and I can't think of a cause better than giving kids the opportunity to grow and learn in school without having to worry about the basic need of hunger. Donate now! Thank you again, and let's get back to the bake-off."

Lexi sniffled, surprised to feel the tears on her cheeks. What was it about this man that could make her furious one minute and sobbing the next? At least this time, the tears were for the small amount of remorse she'd seen in him.

She told Charlotte she needed a few more minutes to compose herself and her thoughts. Emotions seemed to bounce off every surface they could find within her. A few minutes later, she emerged, the crew finalizing the setup on the stage. When one of them passed her, she asked, "We aren't filming in the big classroom?"

The man shook his head. "No, Miss Charlotte said there are too many people already, so we should set up out here."

The crowd in front was loud and big. From her spot on the side of the platform, she could see line after line of people filing in. Cameras milled about, and she hoped all of this had been worth it for her favorite organization. All the emotions, all the special moments in and out of the kitchen. Her time with Brennen.

She kept to the shadows as she watched Brennen set up

his station, proud of how far he'd come in such a short time. Pulling out her phone, she got a message from Sarai saying she'd sold out of every item they had in the truck and had to close already. She looked up at Brennen, the wall around her heart softening in spots.

Brennen looked around and part of her hoped he was searching for her. She wanted to rush out to him, to have him hold her, kiss her, and wipe away her Dateless Woman nickname forever. But something held her back, an inner emotion that wasn't ready to break down all her defenses just yet.

The timer began, and she knew she couldn't make an entrance, afraid to throw off Brennen's concentration. She'd wait until she could control her emotions.

Lexi was impressed with Jessica's baking skills, but after all she'd heard the woman say over the past few weeks, Lexi was grateful she'd been paired up with Brennen, near-shattered heart or not.

He'd been so focused on the task at hand, he didn't look around again, not until he began the pastry cream. She stepped out of the shadows at last, claiming the last empty seat behind the judges. The joy on Brennen's face when he saw her enter made her heart soften even more, and she was glad she'd come today. Her feelings were still all out of whack but at least she wouldn't regret staying away.

The bell sounded, signaling the end of the competition.

"Contestants, please bring your dishes up here." The judges stood behind a small table, two cameras trained on them from different angles.

She craned her neck, trying to see how Brennen's final piece turned out, but he stood in the way. The tall, toned form of his back made her wiggle a little bit, and she pulled her eyes away.

Jessica had gone with the macarons, the elegance of the

entire piece was stunning. She'd stacked them all together to form the Eiffel Tower. With the elegant gem pieces every so often, Lexi knew Brennen would have to be flawless to pull off a win.

"These look like they've been prepared well. Good execution for this tower, Jessica. Brennen, this is an interesting piece. Would you care to tell us about it?"

* * *

WITH THE CAMERAS in his face, sweat beaded up on Brennen's forehead. He thought it had been rough to have the press conference earlier, the shaking of stepping into the public eye with all the attention on him had caused his body to shake. But now, especially since Lexi was in the room, his nerves took over, making him wonder if he'd done the right thing. He only had one more chance to apologize and ask her forgiveness.

"I made a large food truck out of picarones. It's a popular dessert from Peru, where my coach's family is from originally. I made it because judging something like a food truck is as bad as not giving a person a chance because of your first encounter. Someone special taught me that."

He didn't know where the other camera had gone, but he was glad that part was over. The judges cut into his masterpiece, taking a small bite. They made several comments, most of the words sounding familiar now after seven weeks of baking. But his brain was concentrated on the girl behind him, hoping beyond hope that she would forgive him for lying and see that he really was the person she'd gotten to know.

Charlotte spoke up from the side of the table. "We thank you and all of our sponsors for this first annual bake-off for Project Fed. We got word this morning that someone will be matching all donations for the charity so make sure to get those last donations in before the end of tonight. Right now, let's look at the numbers our viewers have donated."

Someone walked up and handed her an envelope, which she opened slowly, driving Brennen crazy. He had to calm down. Drama and suspense increased ratings, even if it were just a local station, and that's what they would do to announce the winner.

"We've raised double our goal already at fifty-thousand dollars. Meaning with our anonymous donation, we will be able to give one hundred-thousand dollars to feed the kids of Boston this summer and hopefully into fall. Thank you! When we came up with this idea, we didn't think we'd have this kind of response." She paused for a moment and then said, "I'm getting word that #Bostonbakeoff is trending on social media, so please share all you can. There are plenty of places to donate, and you can continue to help out Project Fed long after this competition is over."

Loud cheers went up around the room, and they all smiled, the wait almost killing Brennen.

"Judges, have you made your decision?" Charlotte's voice brought him back to the present.

Sylvia stepped forward and said, "We'd like to congratulate our semi-finalists for an amazing job of both execution and creativity of their bakes. We need to have a winner and for bringing heart to the piece, as well as great flavor, Brennen Peters is the winner!"

It took a few seconds to register, but he smiled, allowing the judges to hug him for a moment. When he turned around, he found Lexi over by the other pro bakers, past and present. She seemed nervous, something he wasn't used to seeing in her, but the vulnerability was inviting. She smiled at him but stayed in her chair.

He walked up to her, unable to stay away. "I can't believe we won. This is awesome!"

"Congrats, Brennen. You deserve it." So reserved, so cautious. But with her hair all the way down and a more modern sundress, she was breathtaking.

"I couldn't have done it without you. Besides, doesn't that mean you have a chance at Baker of the Year?" He looked down at her, her face scrunched as she thought about it.

"I guess so. That's not the most important thing in my life right now though. I can't believe you made a food truck out of picarones. Why?" She shook her head, a hint of a smile on her lips.

As per usual, Charlotte interrupted them.

Darn it, woman! Leave us alone!

"They need you for an interview, Brennen." She pointed to the cameras and a chair set out in the corner of the stage.

"Good luck, Brennen," Lexi said, moving toward the stairs of the stage. He tried to call out to her, but Charlotte pulled him back.

Plan D it would have to be then.

Pulling a card out from his back pocket, he handed it to Charlotte. "See that Lexi gets this, will you?"

Charlotte looked at it with a curious expression. "What's this for?"

"To tell her I'm sorry. Give it to her before she leaves."

He finally turned to the cameramen, hoping his plans worked out. He wasn't about to lose the woman he loved. It was all up to her now.

CHAPTER 32

"Do you want to grab dinner in a bit?" Lexi turned to see Charlotte standing behind her.

"I'd love that. But don't you have to clean up around here? There's a lot to do."

Charlotte smiled at her. "Yeah, but it will go faster with another pair of hands. Help me, and then we'll go get something. Will you organize the papers to send to the sponsor companies? They're in my office."

Lexi was grateful to be tucked away in the back of the school. The office was so quiet, such a change from the loud crowd moments before. It didn't take long to get a system down to organize the papers, and she was grateful for something to do that didn't take much brain power. She was zapped and probably would be for the next few days. Weeks even.

She pictured Brennen's face as he wanted her to celebrate the win with him. But it was better this way, better she hadn't reached out and touched him. He might have gotten over it in a few days, but she knew herself, and her mind wouldn't let her forget so easily.

Two hours after the end of the competition, the building was almost silent, and Charlotte announced she was ready to go. Lexi had fallen asleep in the chair behind Charlotte's desk and was in the sleeping fog that came with a long sleep in the middle of the day.

"Are you ready to eat? I could go for a whole side of beef." Charlotte smiled, picking up her purse.

"Yeah, what do you feel like? My stomach isn't giving suggestions at the moment."

The two of them piled into Charlotte's SUV, and Lexi was grateful to not have to take the T all the way into town and home. It hadn't been bad on the days when she didn't have her car but after the ups and downs this day had dealt her, she was grateful for that small blessing.

Charlotte talked every now and again, but Lexi felt like she was constantly clearing cobwebs from her brain. By the time they made it through traffic and downtown, she was wide awake.

"Why are you going into the city? It's Saturday night. The restaurants will be packed." Lexi frowned. She'd just dealt with a whole crowd of people, and she wasn't in the mood for that again.

"There's this place I've been wanting to try out, and who better to go with than my partner in crime?" Charlotte winked at her, and Lexi rolled her eyes.

"Where is it?"

"If I tell you, it'll ruin the surprise."

Lexi stretched out her hands. "Do you see all these people? They're all looking for someplace to eat, and they've taken up all the parking spots."

Charlotte pulled to a stop along the curb, the red paint coated the length of the block. "You can't park here, Char. Tow away zone."

"It's a good thing I'm not parking then, huh?" She handed

Lexi a small card. "Take this to the hostess stand, and they'll direct you where to go."

Turning to look out the window, Lexi's eyes went wide. "I'm supposed to eat by myself at Top Shelf? How did you even get a reservation?"

"I'll tell you all about it later. It's a perk of the bake-off, and you should have it."

She got out of the car and gave a weak wave to Charlotte as she pulled away from the curb and sped off. A man pulled the door open and waved her to walk through. She thanked him and felt a rush of emotions flood through her. She was going to eat here.

By herself.

That put a damper on things. She'd done a lot by herself in the past, and it hadn't bothered her. But now, she felt that emptiness in her chest.

Once inside, the smell of spices filled her nose, and she looked around. The restaurant was packed. She looked up at the chandelier hanging in the middle of the restaurant with several smaller ones spaced out around the rest of the ceiling.

A girl looked up at her from behind the hostess stand. "Do you have a reservation?"

Lexi lifted the card to the woman, realizing she hadn't had the time to even look at it. The girl smiled at her and said, "Right this way."

Only a few steps behind, her senses tried to take in everything all at once, as if this were her only chance to fill up on the beauty and ambience of it all.

The girl led her to a room in back, which held only a handful of tables, all empty. As she took a seat, her mind tried to piece together the last fifteen minutes. The place she'd always wanted to try, and here she was without anyone to share it with. She pulled out her phone, half-wishing Brennen would call or text.

In the room walked a large blond man. His shoulders had to be the width of a door. "Good evening, Miss Sargento—"

"Sarmiento," Lexi said with a laugh. The man made a face and then smiled. As she studied his features, he looked familiar, and she couldn't pinpoint from where.

"My name is Carson, and I'll be helping you out tonight."

Lexi pointed at him. "Carver. Carson Carver, right? From the Boston Breeze?"

He smiled wide. "Guilty. I own the restaurant, and sometimes it's fun to pretend I'm a waiter. What would you like to drink tonight?"

"Water." Her mouth was parched from the long day, and she needed to rehydrate.

"Are you sure? We have an entire restaurant with a full bar." Carson looked to Lexi, eyebrow raised.

She shook her head and gave him a close-lipped smile. "No, I'm good for tonight, thank you."

Carson disappeared behind the door, and some classical music began to play. He came out a few moments later with a salad and a large glass of water.

As he turned to leave, Lexi said, "Do you have a menu or something?"

"Ah, usually yes. But your meal has been chosen for you. It should be out in a few minutes. Please let me know if you need anything while you wait."

"Do you have to go? I don't want to eat alone." She felt her face flush and hoped the dim light covered at least part of it.

He sat across from her. "I could probably sit for a minute."

The silence was so awkward, she stabbed her fork into the lettuce leaves, trying to be as ladylike as possible.

"So, Miss Sarmiento. What brings a pretty gal like you in by yourself?"

She narrowed her eyes at him, trying to decipher if he would be a good sounding board or not. "I like a guy, but he lied to me about part of his identity. It triggered all sorts of feelings and memories from a bad relationship years ago, and I was frustrated." The condensed version of the past seven weeks didn't seem as tragic as she'd felt earlier. To his credit, Carson was a good listener.

The door opened, and a tall, thin man with shaggy gray hair to his chin walked in, holding two plates. Lexi smiled at the man, but it seemed to stop halfway as she put his face into the catalog in her mind.

"Pierre Roux?" Her voice was little more than a whisper.

How did the bake-off pull all these strings?

"Oui, mademoiselle. It is a pleasure to serve you tonight. From what I've overheard, you're a talented baker. I have tried to talk to the owner on several occasions to hire a pastry chef. I'm sure our patrons would love to sample from the desserts you make."

Lexi gulped, pinching her arm beneath the table. Was this really happening? She was meeting the man she'd idolized over the past few years, binge watching all the reality shows he'd starred on.

"I, well, I own a food truck. I do some catering, but I haven't been the head pastry chef ever. I worked at La Crème as an assistant pastry chef for a few years." She was babbling. Why couldn't she just stop already?

"An ambitious girl. I like her already." Pierre bowed and when he straightened, he said, "Welcome, and it was so nice to meet you. For tonight, we have a rosemary and garlic roast beef with brown butter scallops and a side of parmesan risotto. How does it look?"

Never breaking eye contact, Lexi said, "Wonderful. Thank you."

"Please let us know if you need anything. We'll just be in the kitchen." He looked over at Carson and thrust his thumb toward the door. Carson reacted, scrambling out of his seat and disappearing again. It was only then that Lexi realized Pierre had brought out two plates, one in front of her and one sitting across from her.

She paused, wondering what she was to do, but the aromas of the food wafted up, causing her stomach to growl with hunger. Her knife sliced right through the beef, and the flavors flooded her mouth. Just as she was about to take another bite, the door opened.

Turning her head, her breath caught in her throat, surprised to find Brennen's face. He closed the door and walked towards her, the navy-blue slacks and salmon-colored polo shirt accentuating the muscles hiding beneath. She felt herself gulp and as hard as she tried to tear her eyes away, she couldn't.

He stood next to the chair Carson had vacated moments before and asked, "Is this seat taken?" With a hesitant smile, he raised one eyebrow, causing Lexi's insides to simmer.

With a slow shake of the head, Lexi stuffed another bite of meat into her mouth and met his gaze. When she'd swallowed, she asked, "Did you do all of this?" She waved her fork around the room.

His face was somber and vulnerable. "Yes."

"Why?"

He laughed but without feeling. "Why would I do all of this? Because I'm sure you're the girl I want to spend the rest of my life with."

Her mouth dropped open, and her hands started to sweat. What would she say to that?

"I love you, Lexi. I think I started to the day I met you at speed dating. There have been so many components to what makes you tick, and I love learning about all of them. I know we've only known each other a short while, but you're one of the most amazing, kind, and feisty girls I've ever known. I want to be the one to hold you when you cry, not be the cause of it. I want to go to every restaurant in town and watch you detect every spice and flavor. And I for sure, want you by my side, helping me be a better man. What do you say?"

With no words coming to her, she pulled the napkin from her lap and slid out from her chair. She took one long step and stood in front of him, her wedge heels helping cover some of the height difference. Their eyes locked, and she went on tiptoe, her lips touching his in a sweet caress. She reached up with her hand, wrapping it around his neck and pulling him down a few inches, crushing her lips to his.

Her thoughts tumbled around in her head, and she wondered if this was just an amazing dream. She parted her lips, and he deepened the kiss, wrapping his strong arms around her and pulling her to him. His fingers combed through her hair and a few seconds later, he pulled back, resting his forehead on hers.

"You didn't answer my question."

"That was, uh, pretty great." She giggled. Moving so she could whisper in his ear, she said, "I think I'll keep you around forever. Should we enjoy this meal as a party of two?"

Five months later, Lexi walked out of the tent that housed her gingerbread creation. Her stomach threatened to lose its contents, and she wanted to run from the room as she saw several news cameras making their way down the line of entries.

She'd been given number twenty-six out of twenty-eight contestants, and she didn't want to think about her odds for winning.

Glancing around the large room at one of the hotels up in New Hampshire where the final event was held, Brennen was nowhere to be found.

He'd told her all those weeks ago that he would be there to hold her when she cried and right now, she was at the breaking point. Her nose hurt, signaling the formation of tears in her eyes. Wrapping her arms around herself, she needed to breathe and get through this moment.

When the camera crew arrived, she smiled, trying to understand the reporter's words. Lexi could speak two languages but whatever the woman said, wasn't something she comprehended. An arm wrapped around her waist, and she looked up to see Brennen, his face a bit flushed and his eyes bright. He leaned down and kissed her, easing the panic that had built up in the last few minutes.

"Lexi Sargento—"

"Sarmiento." Her tone added more confidence, and she looked at the woman, recognizing her as that Susie woman from the *Everything Your Heart Desires* show.

As if not hearing Lexi's comment, Susie continued, "What is it you've baked for the judges?"

Taking a step into the tent, she couldn't help but smile as she looked at the large edible creation. "My food truck."

The woman's eyebrows became one and she said, "A food truck? Why is this so important to you?"

"It was my passion, my sole focus in life. I hid behind it as I ran from my problems." Lexi pushed the button on the wooden base of the gingerbread food truck. "But when I realized that love could conquer a lot of things, my life started again."

Tiny Christmas lights glowed around the outside of the truck and on the inside, she'd placed two people made of modeling chocolate, one at least a head shorter than the other. They stood, smiling, with a pastry in their hands.

"Isn't that... cute?" Susie's nose turned up, and Lexi laughed.

"It's not for everyone, but that's how our story began." Lexi turned to look at Brennen but found him on one knee on the floor of the tent, something small in his outstretched hand.

"Alexis Sarmiento, plus the four other names you never use," a hint of a smile around his lips made her grin. "Will you help me continue that story and become my wife?"

She paused for a second, and his face fell, as if he'd been worried about rejection all along. Pulling him up, she put her mouth next to his ear and said, "Yes."

He whirled her around, only stopping to pull her in for a kiss. It was then she realized the crowd that had gathered outside her tent.

"Charlotte? Mami? Papi?" She looked around at their happy faces. All her sisters were there, Meg, Parker, and even Jessica Pace and her family.

They each gave the newly engaged couple a hug, and Lexi was sure her face would split from smiling so much. Brennen held onto her hand and when he leaned over and she smelled his delicious scent, she couldn't help thinking he would be hers forever. He said, just loud enough for her to hear, "Peters, Party of Two."

She didn't care what happened with the competition at that point. Because she'd gotten the best grand prize of all. The love of her life.

* * *

Continue the *Love, Austen series* with Ruby & Carson's story in *Austen Unscripted.*

* * *

Thank you for reading *Austen, Party of Two!* If you enjoyed it, I would love to see a review from you. You can also subscribe to Britney's newsletter here:
Subscribe to Britney's List
Or join her Facebook Reader Group

ALSO BY BRITNEY M. MILLS

The Love, Austen Series
Love, Austen
Austen, Party of Two
Austen Unscripted
Matched, Austen
Austen, Edited
The International Billionaire Series
The Australian Billionaire
The French Billionaire
The British Billionaire
The Vegas Billionaire
The Italian Billionaire
Rosemont High Baseball Series
The Perfect Play
The Perfect Game
The Perfect Catch
The Perfect Steal
The Perfect Hit
Christmas at Coldwater Creek Series
Love in a Blizzard
Love in the Lights
Love in a Snapshot
Love in the Details
Sage Creek Small Town Series
Loving His Flower Girl

Loving His Reporter Girl

* * *

Join Britney's newsletter

Get the latest updates on new releases and other fun tidbits!

www.ingramcontent.com/pod-product-compliance
Lightning Source LLC
Chambersburg PA
CBHW021334190726
48288CB00003B/1106